SUMMER IN HANOVER SQUARE

The impoverished Margaret Lambart is suddenly flung into all the glitter of the Season in Regency London. Suspected by her godmother's nephew, the influential Marquis St. George, of being merely a common adventuress, she has, nevertheless, a brilliant success, and attracts the attentions of the young Duke of Oxford. However, when the Marquis discovers that Margaret is far from wanting a husband he finds he has to revise his estimate of her true worth.

CHARLOTTE GREY

SUMMER IN HANOVER SQUARE

Complete and Unabridged

LINFORD
Leicester

First published in Great Britain in 1981 by
Robert Hale Limited
London

First Linford Edition
published 1999
by arrangement with
Robert Hale Limited
London

British Library CIP Data

Grey, Charlotte
    Summer in Hanover Square.—Large print ed.—
Linford romance library
    1. Love stories
    2. Large type books
    I. Title
    823.9'14 [F]

    ISBN 0–7089–5485–5

Published by
F. A. Thorpe (Publishing) Ltd.
Anstey, Leicestershire

Set by Words & Graphics Ltd.
Anstey, Leicestershire
Printed and bound in Great Britain by
T. J. International Ltd., Padstow, Cornwall

This book is printed on acid-free paper

1

As the bridal carriage bearing her youngest sister away for the customary wedding-tour turned out of the gate, Margaret Lambart heaved a silent sigh of relief. There had been pearls and white satin and lace veils enough at Jane's wedding; no one would be able to say that she had done less for her youngest sister than for the other three, and Margaret felt justifiably proud of herself.

For there had been a constant struggle to find sufficient money these last ten years since their parents had died, and a price had been paid, not least by Margaret herself; but her duty was done now and she was entitled, she thought, to indulge for once in a little self-satisfaction: after all, her four sisters had all married very creditably, and this last one, Jane, the most creditably of all.

And Margaret had provided a dowry for each of them of which they had no need to be ashamed, and they were all more than respectably settled in life.

She glanced quickly at the two sisters now standing near her, waving after the departing carriage. She could guess exactly what their thoughts were, or soon would be — immediately the carriage was out of sight: 'Poor Margaret! Quite alone now. Poor Margaret! I feel so sorry for her. We will ask her to spend next Christmas with us; the children can be kind to her then, she will like that, and it is not necessary for her to come for a long visit. There is no need to see much of her. Yes, yes, that will be best; it would not do at all to take her to Scarborough with us this summer, for really she is so exceedingly uncomfortable with fashionable people. Poor Margaret, she always looks so drab! I should hate to dress so. Poor Margaret — so dull, so unfashionable — it is a great shame, but, really — she has no style!'

Her brothers-in-law, at least, two of them, would think much the same: 'Poor Margaret — an ageing spinster — why, she must be now at least twenty-seven! — and there could be only a very moderate portion — there was very little hope, if any, and it would be very awkward if she came to expect to depend upon them. They had their own families to consider and really Pettigrew was very lucky coming from such a distant part of the country!'

As these thoughts were running through her mind, her sister Sarah sighed sentimentally.

'You will feel very lonely now, I expect, Margaret,' she said, and looked at her eldest sister with a good deal of easy pity.

Margaret did not answer, but hiding a rather grim little smile, she continued to wave till the bridal carriage bearing her youngest sister, the new *Lady* Pettigrew, wife to Sir Thomas Pettigrew of Caerdew in the County of Cornwall, was out of sight. Her other sisters had made prosperous marriages, but none quite the equal of this: Elizabeth, the middle sister, was married to Mr Milton Fawkes-Millar, who had a small estate in Derbyshire; Sarah, next to the youngest, was the wife of the Reverend Arthur Temple, nephew and heir to the local squire, Sir Brooke Fortescue, and vicar of Emberley, their neighbourhood parish; and Anne, next in age to Margaret herself, was the wife of Mr James Thornton, a local gentleman-farmer, who, at the time of the marriage, had been considered the most eligible *parti* in their quarter of Cheshire. Yes, all in all, Margaret felt she had done very well for her four younger sisters.

Margaret had borne the burden of responsibility for the family ever since her parents had been killed in a carriage accident when she was just seventeen. This had meant that, instead of enjoying the delights normal to a young woman: balls and parties and visiting friends and meeting possible suitors, she had had to take her parents' place and bring up her four sisters on a greatly reduced income and with little help but for their faithful old retainer, Tabitha, who had been the nurse of all of them in turn. Selflessly, she had put aside all thoughts of marriage for herself till her sisters were grown and suitably settled in the world. This had not been the only sacrifice, even if the major one. She had always denied herself a dress or a pleasure if her sisters' needs conflicted with her own, and in consequence her sisters had always come to expect this. Margaret was aware that this was entirely her own doing, but her nature had prompted it as a duty.

The bridal carriage was now out of sight, and Margaret and her sisters and brothers-in-law turned back to the house.

'Poor Margaret,' said Sarah with a heavy sigh, taking her sister's arm. 'You will be feeling things very much now.

I do wish it were possible for you to come back to the vicarage with us. I do not like to think of your being here all alone. But you know we have the Dysons dining with us, and I expect you would prefer to avoid company at this time.'

'Indeed!' murmured Margaret absently with a vague smile, brushing rice grains from her lace cuffs.

And that had been all she had said till some time after they were returned to the drawing-room. They could hear Tabitha already clearing away the remains of the wedding-breakfast in the eating-room. The cousin who had been Sir Thomas's groomsman had already ridden off to Cheadle on the first stage of his long journey back to Cornwall, and Elizabeth had been unable to be present because of a certain condition, so that there were just the six of them there when Margaret had dropped her thunderbolt.

Her brother-in-law Milton, truly fond of Margaret and therefore the member of the family who was perhaps the most concerned for her now, had been trying genuinely hard to persuade her to return to Derbyshire with him.

'Elizabeth will like to have you with her at this time,' he had said.

Margaret had looked up at him and merely said with a smile, 'Dear Milton.'

Anne said, 'What you will do with your time now, Margaret, I cannot think; you will have nothing to occupy you any more.'

'Oh, pray do not worry about me. I assure you, I shall be very busy.'

'Ah, yes,' said her brother-in-law Arthur sententiously, 'I expect you will spend your time in good works, sewing for the poor and visiting the sick. I shall be able to look to you for a great deal of support in my poor work; you will like that.'

Margaret gave him a look, and her sister Sarah added with a smug smile,

'Yes, I have so many other calls upon

my time, and Margaret has such a way with her; she always knows exactly how to talk to everyone. As you know, Margaret, I admire you excessively for it; I simply cannot think how you can support the tedium.'

'I would have thought that sick-visiting was an accomplishment you would have learnt for Arthur's sake,' Margaret answered a trifle tartly.

'Oh, no, sister,' Arthur said portentously, 'there is no need for my wife to busy herself with such matters. I am happy to say that I am in the position where it is more suitable for my wife to keep to the drawing-room.'

'Well,' said Anne, 'I am very glad that Arthur will be able to use your help, Margaret, for otherwise I simply cannot see how you would fill your time.'

'I expect you will be able to play cards with Sir Brooke and Lady Fortescue more frequently now,' said Milton with a kindly smile. 'That at least will be an agreeable pleasure.'

Had it been any other of them who had spoken this, Margaret in her present mood would have been tempted to reply sharply that she did not care if she never saw another card again; as it was, she merely gave him an odd look, but kept silent.

'And of course, dear sister, you are always welcome to walk in our park at any time. I know the river-path at the bottom of our grounds is a favourite one with you,' her brother-in-law James added generously.

'It is very kind of all of you,' Margaret said deliberately, getting up and walking to a pier glass and looking at herself for a moment, 'to be so very concerned about me. Indeed, I am very touched by your obvious anxiety for my welfare, but I am very happy to assure you that there is no need for it. You see,' she went on, patting her hair smooth, and taking a quick glance at each of them in turn, 'I shall not be staying here.'

9

'Not staying here!'

Five astounded voices spoke almost as one.

'Oh, no. I do not intend to remain here. I am going to London!'

Five pairs of astonished eyes stared at her in open disbelief.

'London!'

Margaret Lambart nodded. She looked at the reflections of the five people in the glass. She was indeed pleased with the effect she had created — better, even, than she had hoped. For dull, domestic Margaret to set out for London was an idea totally alien to them, she thought a little grimly. She could not repress a slight feeling of pique as she turned round and faced her family.

'Oh, yes! I fully intend going there,' she said brightly. 'I have already made arrangements.'

'But — for what?' burst out Anne. 'What will you do there?'

'Oh,' said Margaret airily, 'I expect I shall go to balls and to the theatre and concerts — all the things one normally does in London.'

'You!' cried her two sisters together.

'Of course. What else should I do there?'

'But — '

But they were too amazed to protest coherently yet.

'When — er — do you propose to leave?' James enquired rather suspiciously.

'Very shortly. The exact day is not yet decided, but — it will be some time at the beginning of May.'

'You will arrive in time for the beginning of the London season!' Anne burst out.

'Exactly,' replied Margaret matter-of-factly.

'But — but — *you* cannot do the season!' Sarah cried.

'Oh? Why not?'

'Because — because — ' Sarah thought frantically, ' — because it would cost a great deal of money!' she brought out triumphantly.

'I am only too well aware of that, Sarah.'

'But — you have not the money!' Anne suddenly looked hard at her sister. 'Or have you?' she demanded.

'I have a little money left to me now that all your dowries are paid. I intend spending that.'

'But — you are — I mean — '

'Yes, Anne?' Margaret said with interest. 'What *do* you mean?'

'If — if — if there is anything left, it — it should be shared out between us all!'

'What there is *has* been shared out between you all. And I would point out that mine will be the smallest share. So you need have no ill-feeling on that score,' Margaret returned evenly.

'But,' said Sarah returning to the attack, 'it is so very strange — after all these years — I mean — you are — well — '

'What you are trying to say, Sarah, I collect, is that you think I am far too old to be setting out on my first

London season?'

'Well, no — not exactly, I mean — well — yes, you are. You are quite twenty-seven now!'

'Twenty-seven and seven months almost exactly,' Margaret confirmed.

'And — and you know no one in London!'

'I daresay that will soon be remedied.'

'Are you sure this is a wise course to pursue, Margaret?' James now said. 'As Sarah has said, it will be a very great expense, even though you are, of course, unlikely to go to any grand balls requiring expensive gowns, or carriage clothes and so on. But even without these things, London is expensive, and you will not wish to use up all your nestegg in a few short weeks.'

'*We* never had a London season,' Anne said, nursing this new grievance.

'No. And I am very sorry for it, Anne. But it is not something we might have expected, even had Papa not — not died.'

'Then how can *you* afford it now?'

'I have still the money my Grandmother Bankes left me, and with what else remains, I daresay I shall manage. And when it is all gone, and I have no money left, I shall look for a post as a companion.'

'Margaret! You cannot!' they all cried, much shocked.

'Indeed, I can. And I shall. I have no wish to live alone. As you have pointed out earlier, I should be quite by myself here now — but for Tabitha. As Jane is married now, there is really nothing to keep me here.'

'But — *we* live nearby!' Anne sounded affronted and aggrieved.

'But,' said Margaret reasonably, 'you all have your separate concerns — as wives and mothers, in which I have no part.'

'Margaret, my dear,' protested Milton, 'we are always delighted to have you with us.'

'Dear Milton, I know *you* are.'

Margaret's inflection was very slight, but it was not lost upon her sisters who had the grace to feel a twinge of conscience, even though it was not enough for them to contradict her next words.

'But I cannot forever be imposing upon you.'

'It is no imposition, dear sister.'

'I know you would not feel it so, but I fear *I* should be conscious of it myself. No, no; it is much better that I should make some provision for my future life.'

'I do not see that it is necessary to go to London for that,' Anne said petulantly.

Margaret drew in a deep breath.

'I do not mean this in any unkind way,' she began, 'but as you are aware, for the last ten years I have given myself up entirely to looking after you four girls. For ten years now I have had to scrimp and save and scheme — not to keep us from starvation, for I thank God we have had enough to save us from that — but to provide new dresses and ball gowns and bonnets, and to hire the chaise from the Bull, and to give you vails enough when you went away, and all the other hundred and one expensive little items that swallow money but which are so necessary for young ladies just out. You will note that *I* have not had a new dress for the last six years; you will recollect, Anne, that I first wore this dress at your wedding, and it has appeared upon three occasions since. It may, of course, make for dowdiness, which I know you do not like, and I am sorry if you have had occasion to be ashamed of me, but at the moment it is the best I have. Further, as I mentioned before, I have provided dowries for all four of you which, in the circumstances, I do not think have been ungenerous.'

She looked from one to other of her brothers-in-law, and they all had the grace to shake their heads. And just as well, thought Margaret grimly.

'Well,' she ended, her voice still light and pleasant, 'I tell you now that I am thoroughly tired of it all, and I want a change.'

The five of them stared at her as if they were looking at a complete stranger. Only Milton seemed to have some gleam of understanding in his look.

'You do not know what you are saying, Margaret,' said Anne in an annoyed tone.

'On the contrary, my dear Anne, I know exactly what I am saying. You have Laidlaw to see to things, but *I* have actually to *do* the housekeeping. Do you think it is amusing? To make gallons of orange wine because we have not money enough to buy French, to contrive how to make the eating-room carpet last another year, to make sure we have spices and sugar and tea enough till Mr Shipley gets his new supply, to make sure the winter meat does not go rancid for lack of salt, and that the moths do not get into the barley, or the mice climb over the mouse tiles and ruin the flour?

17

Would you find it pleasant to have to worry if the bees cannot make honey enough, or the apple trees fail, or if there is not lavender for the polish, or dried dandelions and dock leaves and comfrey and garlic enough for any ailments that may afflict us? It is the very greatest delight, I assure you, to scald a pig, or pluck a chicken, or joint a hare! For Tabitha cannot do everything, and all this, and a great deal more, I have done since I was seventeen. I have contrived new dresses when they were needed for a ball or a picnic, and I have sat up late at night making flats to match those dresses; I have worn the same bonnet for eight seasons now — retrimmed indeed, but still the same old bonnet — because there was not money enough to buy myself one as well as one of you, and I tell you I am heartily sick of it. For a change, I am going to have a new gown, and a new bonnet, and I am going where I shall not have to think of cleaning or cooking or housekeeping! *That*, I assure you, will be delightful and I am much looking forward to it!'

'I cannot think why you have never mentioned anything of this before, Margaret,' Sarah said in a rather petulant tone, 'You have always seemed happy enough!'

'Yes! If you have felt hard done by, why did not you ask us to help you?' Anne added in her aggrieved way.

'I have probably been at fault,' Margaret said evenly, 'but I cannot remember that any of you much cared for household duties.'

Her brother-in-law Milton now spoke in a concerned voice, 'But Margaret, my dear, you cannot go to London alone!'

'I believe the mail-coaches are perfectly safe, Milton.'

Her two sisters looked shocked at the very idea of travelling in a public conveyance, but Milton went on,

'No, no, my dear; I mean, you cannot stay in London alone!'

'Dear Milton, I shall not be alone. I have written to my godmother, Lady James Feniton, and she has invited me to stay with her in Hanover Square. I collect that — '

'Hanover Square!' Anne and Sarah exclaimed together. 'You will be in Hanover Square!'

'That is where my godmother lives,' confirmed Margaret.

'But — that is right in the West End!' cried Anne.

'So I believe,' said Margaret collectedly. She continued, ignoring her sister's scowl, 'As I was about to say, I collect that she leads a very quiet life now. She is, of course, a widow, and her only child Caroline died some years ago, but I know that she lives very comfortably, and at least I shall be free of household chores. I shall take a great deal of pleasure in walking about the streets and looking in the fashionable shop-windows, and I shall go to art galleries and to concerts, and if the fancy takes me, I shall walk in the park at promenade hour to see society drive by. Oh, yes, I expect to enjoy myself very much indeed!'

'You spoke before of balls and routs — and — ' said Anne, still sullenly, but rather more pleased now that it seemed that Margaret did not expect to enjoy quite all the pleasures which London during the season could provide.

'Pardon me, but I did not mention routs. Positively I did not mention routs. In any case,' Margaret added a trifle naughtily, with an amused glance at her sisters, 'I collect that now they are not at all the thing. But, certainly, I mentioned balls; I am positive that my godmother will have some acquaintance who will be giving one, and I have every expectation of at least a ball or two.'

'I suppose you think to find yourself a husband there!' said Anne spitefully.

The other four did look shocked at this, but Margaret answered in a level voice,

'I think you can not have understood

what I have been saying, Anne, but I can assure you, I shall *not* be looking for a husband.'

'You have not seen your godmother Feniton these twenty years, I am sure,' Sarah hurried to say; 'she must be very elderly now. How can you be sure you will agree together?'

'Yes,' Anne put in, 'she must be in her dotage now! She will certainly expect you to wait upon her; you will find yourself spending all your time running to fetch her shawl or her vinaigrette. I can not think you will have an agreeable time at all!'

'From her letters, I would judge Lady James to be very far from her dotage, but I shall see. Even if she is a quite impossible old lady, I am still grateful to her for inviting me to stay with her, and I am fully determined to enjoy my stay in London! It can certainly not be worse than the drudgery I have endured here these last ten years!'

★ ★ ★

Before departing for London, Margaret went to the most expensive and fashionable dress-maker in Chester and purchased a new gown and bonnet. Then she packed Tabitha off to her eldest son in Marple, closed the house, and, attired in her new clothes, and having thrown away her caps, she set out for London some three weeks after her sister Jane's wedding.

'It is far too long since we met,' her godmother cried as Margaret was shown in to the elegant salon in Hanover Square. 'My dear Margaret, you are quite the image of your dear mother.' And as Lady James took hold of both Margaret's hands, she stood on tiptoe to kiss her goddaughter on both cheeks.

'You are very kind, ma'am. I am indeed grateful to you for inviting me to stay with you.'

'Nonsense, my dear! It is I who am delighted to have your company. I see little of my nephews and nieces, apart from St George; they all find me far too old and tiresome once they have made their duty call, and I always tell them that they neglect me quite shockingly. But as, apart from St George,' Lady James went on in a whisper, and with a mischievous smile, 'I do not find them particularly agreeable, their absence does not distress me unduly.'

'I collect that St George is your favourite,' said Margaret with a laugh, 'but I am not quite sure — is he — ?'

'He is my nephew upon Feniton's side; he succeeded to the title when my brother-in-law, the late St George, died. I am quite sure you will like him exceedingly. He is quite in the fashion, I collect.'

'And *he* visits you often, ma'am?'

'Oh, yes, he comes nearly every day, when he is in London. But he is not yet returned. I do not look for him for another week at least. Oh, my dear,' Lady James went on, patting Margaret's hand affectionately, 'I am so looking forward to having a young face about the house. Since Caroline — '

and here Lady James's blue eyes filled with tears, ' — you never met her, of course, but she would have been exactly of an age with you if she had not — ' Lady James shook her head and blinked back her tears. 'Well, now, I must say, my dear, that I am thankful indeed that you have at last decided to think a little of yourself instead of sacrificing yourself so continually to those selfish sisters of yours!'

'Oh, no, ma'am!' protested Margaret. 'They are not exactly — selfish. It is just that they have been used to think of me — well, rather as an aunt, I think. It does not occur to them that I may not possess an aunt's feelings. You must remember that Jane was only nine when we — when we were left. Her eldest sister must doubtless seem very old to her.'

'Well, I am exceedingly glad that you have married them all off so well,' her godmother went on, looking at Margaret shrewdly. 'The Pettigrews are a very old family, and I dare say your other brothers-in-law are well known in Cheshire, though I must admit, I am unacquainted with the families. But I do wish this last wedding had been your own! I should like to see you settled to a life of some ease now.'

'I do not think Thomas would have cared for that!' said Margaret laughing. 'He is some four years younger than I am, and he always treats me with the same respect that he accords his mother! But in any case, I have no wish to be married, ma'am! Nothing would frighten me more! As I told the others after Jane's wedding, I am sick to death of housekeeping; I want a change from all that sort of thing. The very idea of marrying fills me with horror!'

'But if you were married to a rich man, you would not have to think of housekeeping. You would have a housekeeper to keep everything in train for you!'

'But I do not want even to be the mistress of a household — however large, or rich, or full of servants. I want to have nothing at all to do with anything of that kind. I do not even wish to confer with a cook about what we shall eat at dinner, let alone worry as to whether I can make the roast hindquarter stretch for another meal, or whether there is beef pie and oyster sauce enough if the rector arrives unexpectedly when it is upon the table.'

Lady James laughed. 'I see you have had a life full of incident!'

Margaret shook her head and smiled ruefully.

'It was no laughing matter at the time, ma'am, I assure you!'

'Well, I cannot be surprised that you should be glad to escape such concerns, and I promise you, you will not have anything to do with such things while you are here — but — not to want to marry! Of course you do! Every female wishes to marry!'

Margaret shook her head. 'Then here, ma'am, you have the exception which proves the rule.'

'But — your own husband — children — !'

'I have already brought out four young ladies, ma'am!'

'But — to come to London at such a time! It will be a great waste if you do not make use of such an opportunity!'

'I assure you, ma'am, I do not seek to come to London for that. In any case, such dowry as I have will not attract any of the gentlemen I am likely to meet here, I think. But, ma'am, I had not expected to lead a life very much in society. I had thought you were much retired from it — that you lead a very quiet life now.'

'It is true that I *have* led a very quiet life, but now that you are come, I consider it my duty to bring you out!'

'Bring me out!' Margaret exclaimed, staring at her godmother quite astonished. 'But, ma'am, as I have just said, I have myself brought out four young girls!'

'But never been brought out yourself,

I collect!' exclaimed her godmother triumphantly.

'But — '

'Oh, do not deny me the pleasure, my dear,' Lady James pleaded. 'I have thought about it all a great deal since I knew you were coming here. You are arrived a little early, before the season has begun, but when St George returns, I intend to ask his advice. He will tell us exactly what to do!'

Margaret looked doubtful. 'If that is what you wish, ma'am, I shall be happy to fall in with your plans; but I should have thought that I was far too old to make such a debut!'

'That has nothing to do with it!' cried Lady James. 'You may no longer be seventeen, but you have never been in London before, and it will still be very exciting to go to all the right balls and things, no matter how old you are! And I am looking forward to going with you, and arranging for your gowns and bonnets and — '

'Dear ma'am! I have not money

enough to buy a great quantity of such things!'

'But you must not bother your head about such matters!'

'But, ma'am — !'

'I insist, my dear. You must remember that — I was never able to bring out Caroline, and — and — ' Lady James took a deep breath, and managed to control her trembling voice, 'it will give me a great deal of pleasure to do for you what I had hoped to do for her.'

Instead of replying, Margaret kissed her godmother gratefully. She made no further objections; the old lady was obviously highly delighted with her scheme, and Margaret could not bring herself to disappoint her. Whatever her own misgivings, the kindest course was to fall in with her godmother's plans. When she saw how unsuitable was the role in which she had cast Margaret, doubtless Lady James would soon drop her proposals.

'However, as you are come early,' Lady James was saying, 'it will give us time to have some gowns made. I suppose you are already mistress of the dance? You will not need a dancing master?'

'I do not think so, ma'am,' answered Margaret, struggling to keep her face straight.

'No, I suppose not.' Lady James sounded disappointed. 'I am so afraid you will find it dull here, before the season starts. There are only the card parties, just now; held by those who, like myself, remain in London the year round. I hope you like playing?' The old lady looked very anxiously into Margaret's face.

'Oh, yes, indeed, ma'am!' Margaret assured her. 'But there is just one difficulty.'

'And what is that, my dear?'

'I — I suppose you play rather high, ma'am? A penny is what I have been used to play!'

'A penny!' Lady James gave a broad smile. 'I cannot think what Colonel Fitzpatrick would say to a penny!'

'Colonel Fitzpatrick?'

'I play with him very regularly. He is quite a demon for whist, and is always quite unnaturally lucky. Such cards as he has! He is not a rich man, of course, and I think he depends rather upon what he can make at the tables, but — he is quite the gentleman, I assure you. He is always so charming when I lose to him.' Lady James beamed at Margaret. 'It is very lucky, I think, that he is such an expert player!'

'I shall look forward to seeing him play then, ma'am, but that is all I shall do, for I could not afford to lose — '

Lady James leant across and patted Margaret's hand. 'My dear, please forgive me; I was exceedingly unmannerly. But you are not to worry about the stakes. As my guest I shall, of course, take care of them for you.'

'Oh, but ma'am, I could not allow — '

'Now, we will say no more about it. It is all settled. The only thing I worry about is that you will find it dull being with such elderly people.'

'Dull! But I am accustomed to — Oh, ma'am, I promise you I shall not find it dull at all!'

'Your manners are excellent, my dear, but I know you will be looking forward to some companionship of your own age. When St George comes, he will arrange everything, I promise you! Until then, you must do exactly as you please. I do not usually rise early, but you must take the carriage when you take the air in the mornings, and Hannah shall accompany you, and can act as your maid.'

'Hannah! Who is Hannah, ma'am?'

'Hannah was — Caroline's nurse, and she has stayed with me ever since — I could not bear that she should go. Now she helps me with anything I need. She will be delighted to accompany you, and I know you will like her.'

'But, ma'am, I do not need to put anyone out to accompany me. I shall be able to find my way very well on my own.'

Lady James looked thoroughly shocked.

'My dear Margaret, I could not possibly permit you to go out alone!'

'Not go out alone!' Margaret stared at her godmother, completely taken aback. 'But, ma'am, I am twenty-seven; and I have just travelled all the way from Cheshire alone!'

'That is something that could not be helped, my dear. And in any case, your age is quite immaterial. I do not know what may be the custom in Cheshire, but in London it simply would not do for you to go out unaccompanied.'

Lady James's face puckered, and she looked at Margaret so anxiously, that Margaret protested no more. Nevertheless, she was extremely diverted that anyone should have the idea that she should need a chaperone — she, who had been chaperoning her sisters to balls for the last eight years, and who had become quite accustomed to being given a very comfortable seat on the sofa near the fire amongst all the dowagers, while her sisters were on tenterhooks about their next partners, fearful of remaining wallflowers, and jealous of any sister who might achieve the honour of leading off a set.

'I have never had a maid before,' Margaret said with a smile. 'It will be quite a luxury for me!'

Margaret smiled to herself. Really her godmother was spoiling her. And as for being chaperoned, how her sisters would stare if they knew! As if anything untoward was likely to happen to *her*! Still, all this fuss did make her feel — quite decidedly — almost like a young girl again! It was a remarkably agreeable feeling.

2

If Margaret's sisters had been able to see her even in her first days in London, there is no doubt that they would have been a great deal more envious of her than they were already. Though she was not immediately plunged into what the novelists might call 'a vortex of dissipation', she was immediately plunged into preparations for such a vortex, and though both by nature and training, she was not one to give way to an excess of rash excitement, she did feel a great deal more than her usual animation.

For Margaret fell in love with London from the first. It did not matter to her at all that the season was not yet begun; there was so much to see and to do, and with all the enthusiasm of a young girl she embarked upon its exploration. Merely being in the capital she found a source of delight, and when she remembered the activities her family had assumed she would undertake when she had been left alone, she felt almost like a schoolgirl run away from her master, and she all but skipped along the elegant streets and through the gracious squares with a naughty pleasure.

In all her doings, she found Hannah to be a valuable ally. Acting as Margaret's maid, she had offered several tactful suggestions which greatly improved Margaret's appearance: quite taking away her dowdy look with a more fashionable way of arranging her hair, and with advice on one or two modish accessories, she gave to Margaret's dress a touch of distinction.

It was Hannah who procured copies of the latest fashion-plates for Margaret to study, and who accompanied her when she made her first venture into the Bond Street shops. Upon Hannah's advice, Margaret emerged triumphant with a straw hat in the new madrileño style, a Spanish vest in yellow silk, and a pair of soft green Spanish slippers.

'With all this, Hannah,' Margaret remarked as she surveyed herself in her glass later, 'I must look Spanish enough to confuse even Sir Arthur Wellesley himself!'

They tried the effect of a huge comb in her hair, but Margaret burst out laughing as soon as she saw it, and hurriedly took it out.

Hannah said doubtfully that perhaps her face was 'rather too English' to carry off such a foreign accessory really well.

'What my sisters would say if they could see me now!' Margaret exclaimed, marvelling at her new appearance.

Pleased as she was with her purchases, she was appalled at the cost, and from force of habit she began to calculate rapidly how many pounds of wax candles and tea and sugar she might purchase with the sum. Hannah was thoroughly disapproving of this.

'It does not do for you to think of such things now, Miss!' she said firmly; 'my lady would never have the least idea how much a pound of tea might cost, and it would be better if you forgot all about it, too! If every time you buy a new gown or a reticule you try converting them into sides of beef or quantities of huff paste, you will never get any pleasure out of them.'

'I shall not be buying many gowns or reticules, Hannah; you know I have not money enough for that.'

'Now, you would not wish to let my lady down, would you, Miss?' Hannah asked reasonably. 'She has told me that you have neglected yourself for a long time now, and that I was to see that you had everything needful. Very strict instructions she gave me, did my lady, that you are to be fitted out properly. And I must say that you are coming along nicely,' added Hannah, looking at Margaret with a critical eye. 'Now, Miss, I have made an appointment for you with Mr Ford the mantua-maker in

Burlington Street, and we had best be getting along. Very particular, Mr Ford is, about his customers. Last spring he turned away a very well known lady — I name no names — because she was always late, and the lady had to burst into tears and promise to invite Mr Ford to her next rout before he would consent to finish her pelisse. Not that I hold with that sort of thing, even if the lady was — well, never mind. But the fact is, there is no one to touch Mr Ford for such garments.'

But apart from acquiring the necessary wardrobe, there were countless other diverting things to do. With other sight-seers, Margaret shuddered at the growling lions in the menagerie, and laughed at the antics of the wizened little monkeys. She stood amazed at the splendours of the blue and the rose and the gold drawing-rooms in Carlton House, and admired the performance of the pretty ponies at Astleys. She gazed in awe at the Gothic splendours of Westminster, and felt very melancholy as she stood on the exact spot where poor King Charles lost his head. She stared in astonishment at the new gas lighting in Regent Street which almost turned night to day, and, most exciting of all, and quite the most terrifying, she and Hannah went for a ride on Mr Trevithick's 'Catch-me-who-can', and actually progressed twice round the track at the speed of a good posthorse behind the extraordinary puffing machine which drew the carriages.

Oh yes! There were a great many pleasures to be found in London far more to her taste than sick-visiting and poor-sewing which would have been her lot had she remained in Cheshire.

Hannah also took her on occasion to see the promenade in the park. They went in Lady James's carriage, and had the hood down so that they could see properly. To Margaret's inexperienced eyes, the gorgeous creatures she saw seemed all elegance, and she wondered if she would ever be able to approach their gracefulness, but Hannah was very scornful, declaring them all to be rich cits, if not worse, and therefore not persons of fashion at all.

'You just wait till the season has begun, Miss,' Hannah said firmly, '*then* you will see fashion. Just look at that creature over there; the one in the scarlet shawl; *she* is no better than she should be, I'll be bound!'

Margaret felt quite sorry for the young woman in question, who looked quite personable to her, but she did not dare to question Hannah's dictum; Hannah prided herself on her ability to tell a lady at thirty paces, at least.

'And as for the men,' went on Hannah, 'really I had forgotten what scarecrows one can see! You will have to wait till you meet my lady's nephew, the Marquis St George, Miss; now, *he* is a *real* dresser. Always very quiet and elegant. None of these macaroni trappings for him! He will be an excellent model for you, Miss. You couldn't do better than to confine yourself to gentlemen in his style.'

'I think I shall be very lucky if any gentleman at all condescends to take notice of me, Hannah. I do not expect to be in a position where I may be able to choose to confine myself to any particular kind.'

'When your new clothes are ready, Miss, and you have a little more of an air — it will come, Miss, it will come; that is not to say that you haven't got the beginnings of one already — '

'The only air I have,' Margaret interrupted laughing, 'as you know very well, Hannah, is an old maid's air! Confining myself to gentlemen like Lord St George, indeed! You are well aware, Hannah, that not only am I far too old, but also far too penniless to have any chance of attracting any beau *you* would think desirable!'

'Not at all, Miss. As I have said before, you have come on a good way already since you arrived here — '

'Thank you, Hannah,' said Margaret with a smile.

'And I am in hopes that you will

make a very respectable match before the summer is out!'

'Only respectable, Hannah?' Margaret teased; 'even when I am dressed up in all my new feathers? Oh, you are quite right! I shall never be seventeen again!'

'You could still be very pretty, Miss,' said Hannah simply.

'Could I, Hannah?' said Margaret, surprised and touched. 'But I beg you will not expect anything very great. I do not wish to disappoint you. And in any case, I have told you before, I do not want a husband.'

Hannah vouchsafed no reply to this, but merely gave Margaret a look.

★ ★ ★

Margaret had been in London some three weeks now, and daily she could see that more and more people of fashion were appearing in the streets. Her godmother was clearly very excited at the prospect of the season starting in earnest; she insisted on inspecting all Margaret's new clothes as they were delivered in Hanover Square, and grew more and more impatient for the return of her nephew St George. Margaret hoped, somewhat fearfully, that Lady James was not nursing any particular hopes in that direction; she knew that the marquis was not married, and realized that he must indeed be fashionable, as both Lady James and Hannah were constantly insisting upon it, and — they did seem to bring him into their conversations with her exceedingly frequently. Still, Margaret comforted herself, if he was even half as fashionable as they claimed, he would certainly not be interested in anyone like herself, without youth, or great birth, or substantial portion. Nevertheless, she had to admit to herself that she did feel a certain curiosity about him; he might even share her own amusement at the idea of her making her debut at such an advanced age!

Margaret had already met a considerable quantity of people at the evening card parties to which she accompanied her godmother. But, as Lady James had said, they were attended by mainly elderly persons, and however often Margaret assured her godmother that she enjoyed playing whist, Lady James constantly bewailed her inability to provide younger companionship for her god-daughter.

'I do hope St George will arrive soon! I really had expected him before now,' Lady James repeated yet again, looking worried. 'The season has begun at last; I cannot think what is keeping him!' She looked at Margaret piteously. 'I was depending upon him entirely, you know!'

'Oh, pray, ma'am, do not upset yourself. I assure you, I am enjoying myself greatly.'

'But — you have no invitations to balls! You cannot have a season without attending balls!'

'Truly, ma'am, I am very happy!'

'If he does not come by the end of this week, I shall write to him! He will be able to procure all the right invitations for us. Oh, I blame myself very much that I have not taken more part in society these last years!'

In the event, however, Margaret received her first invitation without the good offices of the marquis.

Margaret had seen a notice of an exhibition in a gallery just off Hanover Square. This particular morning was showery, and not having anything else to do, Margaret decided to see the paintings. As Hannah was engaged in some sewing for Lady James, and as the gallery was only a few yards from the square, Margaret dared to venture out alone, hoping her godmother would not notice her from her boudoir window. She had not liked to bother the coachman to have the horses put to for such a short journey, but even though the distance was very little, fat raindrops were already beginning to fall again as Margaret reached the gallery entrance.

It was immediately clear that a great many other people were seeking shelter in the same place. The gallery was very warm, and the air was quite steamy from drying umbrellas; so much so that Margaret soon found that she could hardly breathe. And as for seeing the pictures, what with the tall feathers in the ladies' bonnets, and the beaver hats of the gentlemen, it was a matter of great luck if she caught sight of much more than a patch of painted sky or a monstrous gilt frame.

After some twenty minutes of craning her neck, standing on tiptoe, and trying to peep round those a great deal larger than herself, Margaret decided that retreat was the only sensibe course, and that she should leave the viewing to another day when the weather did not so uncomfortably encourage artistic patronage. Accordingly, she began to make her way to the vestibule. She was held up several times when the crowd was too dense too allow her to pass, and she was subjected to some unpleasantly close views of the collars and hats of some of the other visitors.

She was caught thus behind a young woman, very fashionably dressed and wearing one of the new spencers in a delicate shade of green. The head with its pretty brown curls turned anxiously from side to side as if looking for someone, and Margaret idly wondered how her husband could have allowed himself to become detached from so delectable a creature. They were moving forward very slowly indeed when suddenly, to Margaret's consternation, the young woman in front of her seemed to waver for a moment, and then, with a low moan, she sank to the ground.

The crowd behind tried to push Margaret forward, but she withstood the pressure as best she could.

'A young lady appears to have fainted, ma'am,' she said to the woman immediately behind her. 'If she could have a little air — '

It was with considerable difficulty

that Margaret was able to clear a little space round the unconscious girl. She took her vinaigrette from her reticule and, supporting the young woman's shouders with one arm, she waved the little box gently in front of the girl's nose. Margaret hoped that some gentleman would offer his assistance, but no one seemed to take the least notice of them, merely walking round them and continuing with their own concerns.

However, in a few moments huge violet eyes opened and looked up at Margaret, at first with puzzlement, and then with some embarrassment.

'Oh, I am so sorry,' a sweet voice said softly, and the young woman essayed a little smile. 'I am afraid I have been very silly. I found it so warm in here.'

'It is indeed airless,' Margaret replied. 'I was just endeavouring to make my way to the door for that very reason. Now, I must ask a gentleman to support you to a seat.'

'No, no!' The young woman looked horrified at the idea. 'I — I think I can stand now. If you would be so kind as to support me — ?'

The girl looked despairingly about her. Not surprisingly she could see very little through the press of the crowd.

'My companion is here somewhere, but I seem to have become separated from her.'

'Pray, take my arm, ma'am, and let me help you. There. Please lean on me. I can well bear your weight.'

The girl looked at Margaret gratefully, and in a few moments Margaret had managed to support her to an alcove where they found some unoccupied seats.

'You have been so very kind,' the young woman panted. 'I do not know how I can ever thank you, Miss — ?'

'Lambart. My name is Margaret Lambart.'

'Miss Lambart. I feel so very embarrassed — to make such a spectacle of myself — I really do not know what my husband will say.'

'Pray do not try to talk, ma'am. It would be best if you sat quietly for a little while.'

'He — he did not wish me to come here,' the girl continued, not heeding Margaret's advice. 'But — ' Suddenly her beautiful eyes filled with tears. 'There is a portrait of my sister here which I was most anxious to see.'

'I daresay that if you return on another day, there will not be such a crush.'

'Oh, I did see it, I thank you.' The young woman's voice was scarcely audible, and the tears, trembling on her eyelids, threatened to spill over at any moment.

'Can you see your companion?' Margaret asked hastily. 'What is she wearing?'

'She — she is wearing a grey pelisse, with black feathers in her bonnet. I can not think how we came to be separated,' the girl answered, making an effort to control her emotion.

Margaret stood up and looked about her. She thought she caught a glimpse of some black feathers some distance away. The head wearing the feathers appeared to be turning constantly, for the feathers were in a continual quiver.

'I think perhaps — over there — '

Margaret looked down with a smile. Clearly, the girl who was seated could see nothing.

'I think your companion may be over there.' Margaret gestured, and noticed that the colour was beginning to return to the girl's cheeks. 'What is her name?'

'Miss Martlet.'

'Do you think you will be all right if you sit here quietly while I go to see if — ?'

'Oh, you are indeed kind, but — '

'Yes?'

'Pray do not go far away! I do not like to be left alone!'

'I shall not go out of your sight, I promise you. Take my vinaigrette, then, if you should chance to feel faint

53

again, you will have help at hand.' Margaret spoke reassuringly.

The girl took the little box and gave Margaret a rather shaky smile.

'I shall not be away long,' Margaret promised.

She made her way towards the agitated black feathers.

'Excuse me, ma'am, but are you Miss Martlet?'

The woman turned round and Margaret saw a very sweet, but at the moment a very worried and pathetic face.

'Yes, I am. But I do not think I have the honour of your acquaintance, ma'am — ' The woman's voice was quite pure.

'No. My name is Lambart, Margaret Lambart. I am just come to find you for your companion became a little faint and — '

The old lady gave a gasp, and put her hand up to her heart, a frightened expression on her face.

'Pray do not distress yourself, ma'am,'

Margaret said quickly. 'The young lady is better now. If you will follow me, I will take you to her. She is seated just over there.'

Miss Martlet followed Margaret anxiously. When she saw the young woman, she ran to her with a little cry.

'My dear! My dear! Are not you well?'

'I am quite better now, dear Marty, I thank you. Miss Lambart has been so very kind as to look after me.'

The girl smiled gratefully at Margaret, and held out the vinaigrette. Margaret took it.

'Thank you. I think perhaps, ma'am, now that you and Miss Martlet have been reunited, that you would be well advised to return home as soon as possible.' Margaret kept her eyes resolutely on the young woman's face. 'It is too crowded here for — forgive me, ma'am, but — but — a calmer atmosphere would be beneficial.'

Margaret had concluded long since

that the young woman was in a certain condition. She spoke now quite firmly, as she might have done to one of her own sisters.

'If you will permit me to call you a carriage — '

'Yes, dear Miss Lambart, you are quite right. This *is* all my own fault. Miss Martlet was very unwilling that we should come, but — but I did wish to see Leonora's — my sister's portrait. My — my sister was killed, Miss Lambart; she was thrown from her horse, and this likeness has been finished after — after — the artist finished it from memory.' The violet eyes filled again with tears. 'I had to see it,' the young woman finished simply.

'I am very sorry to hear that, ma'am,' Margaret said sympathetically. Then she resumed in a practical voice.

'If you will permit Miss Martlet and myself to assist you to the door, ma'am, with your permission I will call a carriage — or a chair if you prefer, but I really do think that you should

56

return home at once.'

'You are quite right, Miss Lambart,' the girl said again smiling. 'But there is no need to call for a chair. My carriage is waiting.'

The girl now rose, and with Margaret supporting her with a strong arm on one side, and Miss Martlet rather less reliably on the other, they managed to reach the entrance. There, after several expressions of doubt, Miss Martlet detached herself and went to find the carriage. The young woman turned to Margaret, and caught hold of her hand.

'Miss Lambart, I can never repay your kindness. To take so much trouble to help a stranger. Pray tell me where you reside.'

'I am staying in Hanover Square at number twenty-four, with my godmother, the Lady James Feniton.'

'Lady James Feniton! You mean she who is aunt to the Marquis St. George?'

Margaret nodded. 'Yet, it is the same.'

'I have not had the pleasure of meeting Lady James,' the young woman continued, 'but of course I have heard of her. I hope you will permit me to call upon you in Hanover Square. Lord St George and my husband are great friends.'

Before Margaret had time to reply, an elegant landau drew up with a coachman and a liveried footman, and bearing Miss Martlet. The young lady thanked Margaret once more, bade her goodbye, and was helped into the carriage. Once settled there, she held out her hand again to Margaret.

'Thank you again, dear Miss Lambart. I look forward to our next meeting.'

And with that, the carriage moved away.

It was only when the landau had reached the end of the street and was just turning into Hanover Square that Margaret realized that she had not the least idea who the young woman was, or where she came from.

She walked slowly back to her

godmother's house, thankful to be in the air again, enjoying the sunshine which had now succeeded the rain, and thinking about the young woman who had just left her. It was annoying that she had not been told the girl's name, and she had not even had the wit to look at the arms on the carriage door panels, but the girl had said that she would call at Hanover Square, and Margaret would just have to wait till then. For Margaret had no doubts that the young woman would call.

Meanwhile — she looked about her. Really, London was so beautiful. Margaret looked at the pale green new leaves against the now brilliant blue of the sky and smiled to herself. If she experienced any pang for her lost youth, she was too sensible to dwell upon it.

★ ★ ★

The following morning shortly after mid-day, Margaret was preparing to walk out into Bond Street. She had been told earlier in the week that a new selection of Spanish leather was expected that day, and she had determined to spend a portion of her own money an another pair of soft slippers. She was just in the act of putting on her bonnet when a maid came up to her room, and announced in an awe-struck voice that the Duke of Berrington was below and was asking for her.

'The Duke of Berrington! I know no such gentleman. Was not he asking for her ladyship?'

'Oh, no, Miss. He asked most particularly for you, Miss. Miss Lambart, he said. And what shall I say, Miss?'

The maid was clearly agog with excitement.

'I suppose I had better come down, Ellen, though I am sure there has been some mistake.'

Margaret glanced at herself to see that she was tidy after she had removed her bonnet, then hurried downstairs.

The duke was waiting in the library.

Margaret curtseyed.

'Your grace?'

She saw that he was a man well past his first youth. His hair was going a little grey, but he had an upright figure and a kind and distinguished countenance.

'Miss Lambart?'

'Yes.'

The duke bowed.

'I am come, ma'am, to thank you for the very great service you rendered me yesterday when you assisted the duchess at the art gallery.'

'Oh! Then *you* are the husband — ! Your pardon, sir, but I had no idea of the name of the young lady to whom I was able to be of service. Pray, will you sit, sir? And how is her grace today?' Margaret smiled kindly. 'I trust the duchess is quite recovered?'

'I am happy to say that that is so, ma'am. But I have insisted that the duchess keep her room today. In-er-I-I am afraid she was very rash yesterday, but I do not think any damage has been done.'

'I am so glad. I am afraid the rain caused too many people to crowd inside. There was a great crush, and it grew very warm. I was myself walking to the entrance when her grace was overcome. It was most unfortunate that Miss Martlet was not by her at the time.'

'I blame myself very much, Miss Lambart, that I did not accompany the duchess myself. Unfortunately, I was detained by business; my bailiff had brought me papers that had to be signed at once, and the duchess was exceedingly anxious to go as soon as she could; we have only just returned to London, you see. I think you will know that there is a portrait of the duchess's late sister there. I-I cannot really blame my wife; she is still — very young, as you will have seen.'

'And very beautiful, if you will permit me to say so, your grace.'

The duke's face lit up with his smile.

'You are very kind, ma'am.'

He put his hand into his pocket and drew out a square white envelope.

'The duchess is giving a ball next week, Miss Lambart. It is, I am afraid, very early in the season, and it will not be a large one, because — but I am sure you will understand. But, it would give the duchess and myself very great pleasure if you and Lady James Feniton were able to attend it. I have here cards for you both. Even if you are able to attend for only a short time, I do hope you will come; the duchess would like to thank you properly herself, and I know she wishes very much to see you again.'

'Oh, your grace, how very kind! But I assure you, I was only too happy to be able to help the duchess. I will ask my godmother, Lady James, if she has any engagements for the evening of your ball, and if not, I certainly hope to be present. We — do not go out a great deal, sir.'

'Then I will certainly look forward to

seeing you at Berrington House, Miss Lambart.'

The duke thanked Margaret once again very warmly for the help she had rendered his wife, and then took his leave.

Margaret returned upstairs. She would have liked to have told her godmother of the invitations, but as Lady James rarely appeared before later in the day, she did not mean to disturb her now. She would keep her news till later in the day. However, as she was passing the door of her godmother's boudoir, she was summoned by the older woman.

'Is that you, Margaret?'

'Yes, ma'am.'

Margaret pushed the door fully open and stood in the doorway.

'Come in, my dear.'

Lady James was dressed in a wrapper with a lace cap on her head. She had been writing letters. Margaret entered the room and seated herself.

'Forgive my curiosity, Margaret, my

dear, but — is Ellen correct when she tells me that the *Duke of Berrington* has just waited upon you?'

'Yes, ma'am.'

'I did not know that you were acquainted with him, my dear.'

'I was not, ma'am. But you remember that I told you yesterday about the young woman who fainted at the gallery? Apparently it was the duchess, and his grace called to thank me. He has left us cards for their ball.'

'Their ball!' Lady James stared at Margaret as if she could hardly believe her ears.

Margaret nodded. 'Yes. The duke said that it will be only a small one because — because of the duchess's condition. But, if you will permit it, I would like to attend it, ma'am. I should like to see the duchess again; she was very charming and unaffected.'

'My dear Margaret! Do not you know that — ! No, of course you do not. But the Berrington ball will be one of the most exclusive balls of the season. Even I know that. It has been mentioned several times at the card parties we have attended, but I suppose it did not mean anything to you.'

'No, I am afraid it did not, ma'am.'

'Well, I can tell you that cards are very much sought after. St George will be going, I suppose, but I would never have asked him to use his influence with the Berringtons. They were married only a few months ago; he has always been rather reserved, but Lucy Arrandale was the rage of last season. The duke is, of course, somewhat older than his wife, but he positively adores her, I collect. Before he was married, he was, of course, sought after by every creature with a marriageable daughter, but he never looked at any of them. He was thought to be a confirmed bachelor till he set eyes on Lucy Arrandale for all that she is nearly young enough to be his daughter. There was no holding him then, I am told. So, you have an invitation to their ball! And without anyone's help. Well, you have made a very good beginning, my dear. Now we must plan at once what you are to wear.'

'I had thought to wear the new gown that has just been made, ma'am.'

Lady James waved her hands.

'Oh dear, no; I think you must have something a great deal more fashionable if you are not to feel thoroughly uncomfortable. As it will be a very exclusive gathering, you will not be able to lose yourself in the crowd.'

'But — I have no pretensions to being fashionable, ma'am!'

'There is no reason at all why you should not be. Hannah was showing me some fashion plates the other day, and I think I remember something that would suit you very well. Hannah is very pleased with your improved appearance, but I know she would like you to choose even more fashionable styles.'

'But, ma'am, I have never spent — I

mean, I do not feel comfortable if I spend so much upon my clothes. I am not used to it!' Margaret looked at her godmother anxiously. 'Besides, ma'am, you have been too kind — too generous already.'

'Now, Margaret, we will not mention that! That is all decided; you know it. I insist that we call in Madame Thérèse and bespeak a gown from her.'

'Madame Thérèse?'

'Has not Hannah mentioned her to you? Well, well, perhaps she was waiting till you are more at home here. But I think this is an occasion that calls for one of her gowns. She trained with Madame Berthon in Paris, and has the cut that no one else can match.'

'But, ma'am — ' Margaret began.

'Please say no more, my dear,' her godmother said in a coaxing voice. 'Believe me, you will not enjoy the evening if you are not as fashionable as possible. It would please me so much to see you so,' she added. 'I used to know the duke's mother many years ago now. I remember him as a little boy, but I doubt he will remember me. I shall quite look forward to seeing him again. Well, well; so we are to go to the Berrington ball. I warrant St George will be vastly surprised.'

3

A day or so later Lady James had, very unusually for her, gone out in the carriage at mid-day, and had not told Margaret where she was going, merely saying that she had some commissions to execute; neither had she offered to take Margaret with her.

Margaret was reading quietly in the library when suddenly the doorbell was rung very loudly, making her quite jump. She heard Joshua, the footman, walk across the hall, open the door, and say,

'My lady. Your grace.'

There was the sound of light footsteps in the hall, followed by a rather heavier tread.

'And how is her ladyship today, Joshua?' a woman's voice asked.

'Her ladyship is in excellent spirits, my lady,' Joshua answered.

'We are returned from the country, as you see. No, do not bother, Joshua. We will go straight up.'

'Her ladyship is not at home, my lady.'

'Not at home!' The young voice sounded at first astonished and then rather more suspicious. 'What do you mean? Her ladyship never goes calling.'

'Her ladyship has driven out in the carriage, my lady.'

'Where did she go?'

'Her ladyship did not inform me of her destination, my lady.' Joshua paused. 'But I believe I heard her order Sanders to drive to her jewellers in Bond Street, my lady.'

'Her jewellers! What can she want there?'

Margaret who had been unable to avoid hearing this exchange thought that this unknown female was asking by far too many questions of Joshua, so she rose and went out into the hall.

'Can I help you, ma'am?' she asked.

'Can I give a message for you to Lady James?'

The young woman spun round and eyed Margaret very superciliously.

Now Margaret, at home in the depths of Cheshire, had indeed heard that it was the mode with some ultra fashionable and daring females to dampen their garments so that they clung to the body. When her sisters had giggled over the idea, Margaret had always dismissed it as mere girls' foolishness. 'Think of the discomfort!' and 'Think how cold one must feel!' had been her stock replies. Now she found herself, for the first time, actually looking at a young woman whose garments must have been so treated — they could not otherwise have clung to her form in that way. Margaret felt a hot tide of embarrassment rising within her and she felt quite dreadfully shocked.

'I am the Lady Selina Cumnor, the niece of Lady James Feniton,' the young woman said rather insolently, 'and this is my brother, the Duke of Oxford. I do not think I have had the honour of meeting you before, ma'am?'

Margaret managed to respond equably with only the merest flicker of her eyelids. As she curtseyed to them both, she said,

'I am Margaret Lambart, Lady James's god-daughter. I have but recently arrived here.'

'Indeed!' Lady Selina replied in a voice from which no attempt had been made to remove the suspiciousness. 'I do not recollect Lady James to have mentioned you.'

'Perhaps you would like to await her ladyship's return,' Margaret said, catching sight of Joshua hovering in the background. 'I am afraid I do not know how long my godmother will be, but I will have refreshments brought in for you.'

'Thank you, but that will not be necessary,' said Lady Selina in an icy voice, walking past Margaret and into the library.

The duke gave Margaret a shy smile and waited for her to walk into the room before him. He was a tall, fresh-complexioned young man of about nineteen or twenty, Margaret conjectured, with a friendly countenance in which the colour came and went very frequently.

His sister who would be the elder by a year or two, certainly did not suffer from any such shyness. She was already seated in the wing chair which Margaret had quite clearly just vacated, from the presence of an open book on the table beside it. Margaret seated herself in the chair opposite Lady Selina very composedly; the duke sat down on the very edge of his chair and looked just the reverse.

'You have, I collect, just returned to London, ma'am?' Margaret began.

'Yes, we have been staying in Yorkshire with our kinsfolk the Fenwicks. You do not know the Fenwicks, I collect?' was the impertinent reply.

'No. I am afraid I do not.'

'They have a large estate outside York. We usually spend part of the winter with them — when we leave Bath. The shooting and fishing are excellent. My uncle has some famous coverts.'

'I believe Yorkshire is famous for shooting.'

'Yet, it is. Tell me, Miss Lambart, how long have you been in London?'

'Nearly four weeks now, ma'am.'

'Do you intend making a long stay?'

'I am not quite sure.'

'From what part of the country do you come, Miss Lambart? I do not recollect my aunt to have spoken of a *god-daughter* before.'

'My family is from Cheshire, ma'am. Do you know the county, sir?' Margaret turned to the duke, who so far had not opened his mouth after the initial greeting.

The duke blushed and managed to answer, 'I — I once visited near Ch-Chester, ma'am; I-I thought it v-very agreeable c-country.'

'Yes,' Margaret smiled. 'We think it very beautiful, but then, of course, we are prejudiced. I have spent all my life there.'

'Do not you then go to Bath for the season, Miss Lambart?' Lady Selina asked rather smugly.

'This is the first time I have left Cheshire, ma'am.'

'Indeed!' Lady Selina's eyebrows rose to her hairline, or very near it. 'Do not you find it a very — restricted life, being continually in a country neighbourhood?'

'I suppose it is, had I had time to think about it,' Margaret replied imperturbably. 'But I have four sisters all younger than myself, and after our parents died, I had to look after them. I was always much too busy to bother about what I might or might not be missing.'

'They are all still at home, I suppose?'

There was no mistaking the sneer, but Margaret answered evenly.

'Oh, no, ma'am, they are all married now. The last to marry, my youngest sister Jane, was married last month. That is why I have been able to come to London now.'

'Doubtless you expect to follow your sisters' example while you are here!'

Margaret was so taken aback by this gratuitous rudeness that she hesitated a fraction of a moment before replying. Then she said in her usual composed voice,

'I hardly think that likely, Lady Selina. I have never considered marriage for myself, and I think it rather too late to begin to do so now.'

Margaret smiled as she spoke, for out of the corner of her eyes she had seen the young duke blushing painfully at his sister's question, and out of the kindness of her heart she wished to set him at ease. Now she turned to him.

'You have a house in London, I suppose, sir?'

The young man nodded.

'Y-yes!' he began in a high squeak.

He blushed and started again. 'Y-yes,' he said, a whole octave lower, 'in B-Berkeley Street. It is n-not v-very f-far from Hanover Square.'

'I am afraid I have not yet learnt my way round London very well. I have not ventured far from here.'

'You have done little visiting, I collect, Miss Lambart?' Lady Selina now said. 'I collect that you have not a great acquaintance here?'

'No. I know very few people.'

'And my aunt, Lady James, lives such a retired life!'

'B-but you will soon h-have a host of f-friends, I-I am sure, Miss L-Lambart,' the duke said with some vigour, but a very red face. 'The s-season is only just at the s-start, and when invitations for b-balls and receptions start t-to arrive, you will soon f-find you h-have not time enough f-for all your acquaintance!'

Margaret smiled at him. 'You are very kind, sir. But you draw too sanguine a picture. You must know that Lady James, as Lady Selina has just said, leads such a very retired life that I do not expect at all to be in the social whirl. Nor, indeed, did I exactly come to London for that.'

'Oh?' said Lady Selina coolly. 'Then pray tell me, Miss Lambart, just why you did come here at this time.'

Margaret returned her look, feeling that none of her sisters, for all their faults, would know how to be so rude as this — apparently — well-bred girl.

'It is very simple,' she began serenely, 'as I mentioned before I have spent all my life in Cheshire — I have hardly been outside it. When my youngest sister was married, I simply decided that I would have a change. You, who lead such a very social life, Lady Selina, can never know what pleasure it can give a plain country woman just to walk down Bond Street or Pall Mall and merely gaze at the shops. I daresay that if you are accustomed to visit Bath or Cheltenham or Tunbridge, you are likely to see such things there, too, but I am afraid that the shops in Chester cannot be compared with them for fashion, no matter how hard they try.'

Lady Selina gave a quick glance at Margaret's gown.

'No, I should imagine that would be so,' she said.

'And h-have you seen anything you h-have particularly liked since you h-have arrived, Miss L-Lambart?' the duke asked hurriedly with his usual blush.

'Apart from gazing in the shops, you mean?' Margaret looked at the duke with a good deal of kindness. 'I have enjoyed walking in the park.'

'Oh?' Lady Selina sounded bored.

'Oh, yes, I have seen horses and carriages of astonishing beauty, and a great quantity of charming people, too.'

'Really! You surprise me! It is too early for the ton to be arrived yet. The first ball of any consequence will not be held till next week, but it is very early — for a particular reason.

So I do not suppose you have seen any really fashionable people yet, Miss Lambart.'

'I-I ride in the R-Row every morning, Miss Lambart,' the duke said. 'D-Do you ride, ma'am?'

'Alas, no, sir. I have never had the opportunity to learn.'

'You do not drive either, I suppose?' Lady Selina said. 'I have my own phaeton; it is generally considered one of the most dashing equipages in the park, I assure you. I have cushions to match each gown.'

'Have you indeed, ma'am!'

'Oh, yes. Everyone with any pre-tensions to fashion now has their phaeton. It is quite the thing.'

'Then I am afraid I shall have to remain as unfashionable as ever,' Margaret said with a laugh, 'for I certainly do not drive!'

Lady Selina did not reply to this, but glanced sharply at Margaret, not quite certain whether Margaret were laughing at her or not, but Margaret's face betrayed no such humour. Lady Selina glanced at the clock.

'Really my aunt is a tedious time. Have you really no idea, Miss Lambart, when she will return?'

'I am afraid Lady James did not tell me where she was going, so I have no idea how long she will be. But pray allow me to ring for refreshments for you.'

'No, no, there is no need. I really cannot waste any more time now. I will call to see my aunt later. Come, David,' she went on addressing her brother for the very first time, 'we had better continue with our other calls.'

Lady Selina rose and rang the bell herself. The duke rose also, and blushed again as he observed Margaret take note of his sister's action. The footman appeared.

'We are leaving now, Joshua,' Lady Selina said. 'Pray tell her ladyship that we have called and are sorry to have missed her.'

The girl then walked out of the room.

The duke turned to Margaret with an expression of painful embarrassment on his face. Clearly he wished to say something, but could not think what. From the hall came his sister's imperious voice,

'David!'

The duke bowed deeply.

'Your servant, ma'am,' he said in a low voice.

Margaret gave him a very friendly smile and held out her hand as she curtseyed. Gratefully the duke took it.

'I-I look forward to our meeting again, ma'am.'

'So do I, sir,' said Margaret cordially. 'I will tell Lady James that you are returned to London, and that you and Lady Selina called to pay your respects. I know she will be exceedingly sorry to have missed you.'

'David! Are you coming?' came in annoyed tones from the hall.

Margaret moved into the hall closely

followed by the duke.

'Goodbye, Lady Selina,' she said, and curtseyed.

'Oh. Goodbye.' The girl gave a perfunctory nod, then turned to Joshua who was holding the door open. 'Please give her ladyship my message.'

'Certainly, my lady.'

Lady Selina then walked out.

The duke turned to Margaret, his face scarlet, looked as if he wished to speak, did not, but bowed again and hurried after his sister.

Margaret returned to the library and her book, musing over the very different characters of the duke and his sister.

Lady James soon returned from her shopping expedition, and Margaret hastened to tell her of the visitors. She was quite taken aback by her godmother's reaction.

'Are they indeed returned?' Lady James said with raised eyebrows. 'Now I wonder what Selina could possibly want?'

'How do you mean, ma'am? I had

thought that they had come to pay you their duty upon returning to London.'

'Pouf!' was Lady James's surprising retort. 'You do not know Selina as I do. She would not come here if she did not want something. I am not near fashionable enough for her.'

'But — ma'am — ' protested Margaret.

'You are a dear child,' said Lady James, patting her cheek, 'but that is all you are — a child. Now, did Selina say how long they had been returned to Berkeley Street?'

'I do not think so, ma'am, but I am afraid I do not remember.'

'Well, it is certainly very unlike her to pay me a call — duty or otherwise — very early during her residence here.'

'The — the duke seems to be a very shy creature.'

'David? With a sister like Selina it is hardly surprising, I think. I suppose one should wish that their characters were quite reversed, but as I am very fond of David, I would not like him to be different. He is a dear boy and has a heart of gold, but he is an exceedingly difficult companion. I must speak to St George about him again.'

'St George? Your other nephew?'

'Yes, upon Lord James's side. St George is David's guardian still, and now that the boy has left Eton, he really must take him in hand. I do not suppose St George will care for it, but he ought to take the boy about with him a little, and let him acquire some polish by watching his example. I am writing to St George today; I will mention it then. It is exceedingly vexing that he is not yet returned.'

★ ★ ★

Later that same day Margaret and her godmother were sitting in the small drawing-room when, to their joint astonishment, the Duke of Oxford was announced.

'Dear boy! Dear boy!' Lady James

cried when he was shown in; 'How very kind of you to call again so soon!'

'H-how are you, ma'am?' the duke asked with a blush as he bowed over Lady James's hand; 'You look well, I am happy to see.'

Then he bowed to Margaret. 'Miss Lambart,' he murmured.

Margaret curtseyed.

'I have been telling Lady James that you had called earlier today with Lady Selina. My godmother was very disappointed to have missed you both, were not you, ma'am?'

Lady James gave Margaret a look, then patted the sofa beside her.

'Come and sit next to me, dear boy, and tell me what you have been doing. When did you return to London?'

'We arrived but yesterday evening, ma'am.'

'Indeed! Then I am delighted you were so quick to call. It is quite a new pleasure for me!'

The duke blushed.

'I beg your pardon, ma'am, but I

have not — ' the duke began in confusion.

'Oh, do not be so worried, dear boy! I know you have not yet had the disposition of your own time.'

'We-we were v-very worried by reports we h-had of you, ma'am.'

'Bad reports of me! What can you mean?'

'Selina told me that she had met someone at the Castlefords who had just left London who gave her a report of your indisposition. She was exceedingly worried to hear it, ma'am, and insisted on returning to London full a week earlier than she had intended!'

The duke's speech was strangely free of stammering for once.

'Indeed! I am gratified by her concern. But I cannot imagine what report Selina can have received. I am happy to say that I am, as you see, in quite the best of health.'

'I-I did not hear the report myself — only what Selina relayed to me. B-but I am glad to see that it was quite mistaken. And I-I am very glad that you h-have Miss Lambart with you. It will be better for you not t-to be quite alone.'

'Dear David! I am most curious to know from whom Selina can possibly have had such a report. As you know, I rarely go out.'

'I-I do not know, ma'am, but it was from somebody who had just left London.'

'Who could that possibly be? I have seen no one, except Lady Delaney and Colonel Fitzpatrick in recent days, have I, my dear?' She turned to Margaret. 'And, of course, yourself. Miss Lambart is an excellent card player, David, I am happy to say.'

'I-I am so glad, ma'am.'

'Where did you say Selina met this person? At the Castlefords? You have come from Yorkshire, then?'

'Yes. We were with the Fenwicks. We had a very bad journey, I am afraid. A broken trace outside Market Harbourough, and at Huntingdon we could have only a set of broken-winded nags. Selina was very angry.'

'I am not at all surprised. And no doubt she blamed you. She is busy already, of course. She always has so many people to see when she is here.'

The duke looked very embarrassed.

'I-I think she has gone to c-call upon M-Miss Cholmondelay; and I kn-know I h-heard h-her mention the Duchess of Berrington. Selina is so f-fond of h-her, and was so anxious to see h-her grace.'

'Yes, I am aware of that. I could hardly fail to be. Has she seen anything of St George yet?'

'I-I do n-not think St George is returned yet, ma'am.'

'Well, do not you forget that he is your guardian, still. I do not want to see you go upon the rattle. You could not do better than to follow him in all things,' Lady James said firmly.

'I-I will try, ma'am, but I-I do n-not think I shall manage it v-very well.'

'You must not allow yourself to be

90

overset so easily,' Lady James said in a kindly way. 'Still, I expect when you are St George's age, you will be vastly different.'

'I-I hope I shall be just like him, ma'am.' The duke turned to Margaret. 'H-have you met-h-his lordship, yet, ma'am?'

'I have not had that pleasure, sir.'

'I am sure you will like him exceedingly!' the duke said enthusiastically.

'David thinks he is a very paragon, and I own I am looking forward to playing a hand against him again. Well, when can you come, David? Tell me when I may arrange a table for you. Miss Lambart, I must warn you, plays like a man and gives no quarter. Colonel Fitzpatrick is quite frightened of her.'

'Oh, ma'am,' smiled Margaret, 'your pardon, but you exaggerate!'

'Not at all. I warn you to try to cut Miss Lambart for a partner, David; it is very uncomfortable to see her lay waste a table and not be on her side.'

'And n-not only a ta-table,' the duke managed gallantly, with a warm look at Margaret.

Margaret laughed deprecatingly to hide her surprise, but stopped as she saw the duke's embarrassment. He sat twisting his seal while the colour came and went in his face.

'I suppose Selina will be out in the park this evening,' Lady James now said in the pause that followed.

'I-I think so, ma'am, if she f-finds enough of h-her f-friends are returned.'

'It is still rather early, perhaps. Selina has been rarely returned so soon.'

'W-will you be in the park, this evening, Miss L-Lambart?' asked the duke suddenly turning to her.

'I — have not thought, sir.'

'I — If you would do me the honour, ma'am, it w-would give me great pleasure to drive there w-with you this evening at f-five o'clock,' the duke blurted out with an effort. He managed to look Margaret in the face once as he spoke, but after such an achievement he kept his eyes fixed firmly on the carpet, while even the tips of his ears went pink.

'That is very kind of you, sir,' Margaret said with a quick glance towards her godmother. 'I-er-I-'

Lady James nodded vigorously and Margaret turned back to the duke.

'I should be delighted to accompany you, sir. It will be a very great pleasure. I have been in the park only once or twice with Hannah.'

'Oh, er, yes, H-Hannah,' the duke said, managing a smile but blushing more than ever.

And so it was that some time later Margaret found herself seated beside the duke in his curricle with a tiny tiger behind; the very first time that she had been in such a fashionable vehicle.

Before she had set out, Margaret had expressed some doubts to Lady James about the propriety of driving with the duke, but her godmother had brushed them aside.

'This is perfectly *comme il faut*, my dear,' she said, looking very pleased and pink. 'It is a quite excellent idea, and I do not know why it did not occur to me. You will find it very pleasant, I know, even if David does not talk much and, well, pray forgive me, my dear, but — as you are somewhat older than he is, your driving with him will not signify at all. In any case, as he is my nephew, no one will think anything untoward. It will be a delightful change for you; it cannot be much fun to be playing cards with a lot of elderly people as your only recreation.'

'Dear ma'am, I like it exceedingly, as you know very well! I am always delighted to play cards with you. Besides, when I came to Hanover Square, it was not with any hope of enjoying a great deal of society; I am very content as I am.'

'But I am not content for you. I should exert myself more.'

'But ma'am,' Margaret cried, anxious to see the puckers disappear from the old lady's face, 'people are only just returning to London, it was not possible to do anything before! Besides, there is the Berrington ball next week — '

'To which you are going through no action of mine!' Lady James interrupted, still a little fretful. 'Well, run along now, my dear. You look delightfully in that Spanish hat; I am sure you will turn a great many heads!'

'Oh, ma'am!' Margaret laughed.

The drive to the park was accomplished with very little speech from either of them. Margaret saw at once that the duke was a competent and careful driver, and she settled back to enjoy the drive, watching the bustle in the streets with a good deal of pleasure. When once they reached the park, however, they had to slow down, joining the long line of carriages already moving along the main carriageway.

Margaret turned to the duke, smiling.

'You are very kind, sir. I had never thought to appear here in such a fashionable equipage.'

'I c-can not think why you should s-say that, Miss L-Lambart. I am s-sure there must be a g-great many persons who would be very proud to h-have you beside them!'

The duke was scarlet at the end of this little speech.

'Oh, please do not flatter me, your grace!' Margaret exclaimed with a smile. 'I know so few people in London, that almost no one is aware of my existence.'

'Th-Then you m-must come out m-more often, Miss L-Lambart! You must n-not h-hide your light under a bushel!'

'Oh, but you know Lady James leads a very quiet life, and I am very happy to join her at the card table. You know that is her greatest pleasure, I am sure.'

'I h-have played with my aunt. T-To tell you the truth, she rather f-frightens me at the card t-table!'

'Then I suspect you are not quite

such an — attacking player as Lady James!'

'N-No, indeed, I am n-not! In f-fact, Miss Lambart, I am a v-very indifferent player, and I kn-know my aunt does not care to play with me; but sometimes she n-needs to make up her f-four. But I am v-very nervous, and always f-fear to make a wrong move. You must be v-very expert.'

'I have had the good fortune to play with some very good players in Cheshire. Mr Arbuthnot, he was our rector, and I were often asked to make up a table at the Great House. There is little else to do in the country, sir, so we play a great deal. Apart from my sisters, there were few young people in our neighbourhood.'

'You seem to h-have sacrificed a great d-deal to your sisters, ma'am,' the duke said, turning his warm eyes on her for a moment.

'I did no more than my duty, sir. And now I am having my reward,' Margaret went on smiling, and thinking how very much Anne or Elizabeth would wish to be in her shoes now.

They were able to move forward a little more freely now that they had got away from the crush near the gate. The curricle moved forward at a gentle trot, and soon they were at a little distance from all the other carriages.

The duke suddenly spoke, without turning his head, but keeping his eyes on the track ahead.

'Miss L-Lambart, I-I came to H-Hanover Square f-for the second time today because I-I wanted to apologise to you!'

'Apologise to me! For what, sir, pray?'

The duke took a deep breath and his face — at least what Margaret could see of it, went even pinker.

'I — I am afraid my sister was — was not exactly polite when w-we called earlier today!'

'Oh, please do not mention it, sir; it is of no consequence.'

Margaret was more embarrassed for

the duke than for herself.

'Oh, but it is! I — saw h-how very — patiently you bore what she said. H-had it been you talking in such a w-way, I can assure you m-my sister w-would n-not have been n-near so mild!'

'I have four younger sisters, sir, and I know very well that young people are often very thoughtless, your grace. I have heard my sisters say things which I myself would blush to have said, but they had no intention of being ill-natured. They merely spoke without sufficient reflection.'

'You w-were exceedingly forbearing, Miss L-Lambart,' the duke said, turning to look at her quickly. 'I kn-know my sister w-well enough to kn-know that she h-had every intention of — of being offensive! Selina did not speak w-without thought, but after too much! It is a w-wonder to me, Miss L-Lambart, that you have agreed to drive w-with me!'

'But, why should not I, sir?'

'Because Selina is — my sister, ma'am.'

'And what has that to do with anything? I have already told you, sir, that I am extremely glad that you did ask me to drive in your curricle. It is a pleasure I should not otherwise enjoy. Please do not let us mention this again, I beg you.'

'V-very well. But — I h-had to apologise to you, Miss L-Lambart.' The duke was silent for a few moments, staring ahead. 'W-will you do me the honour of driving out again with me, ma'am?' he asked at last very quietly.

'Thank you. I shall be delighted, your grace,' Margaret said with a friendly smile.

The duke smiled back, and Margaret noticed again how his whole face was illuminated by it. But the duke did not take his eyes from Margaret's face, and after a few moments she felt she must recall his attention to his surroundings.

'I think someone in that carriage

was acknowledging you, your grace,' she cried as a very elegant phaeton and four went by.

'Oh? W-were they? I did not n-notice them,' the duke returned, still keeping his eyes fixed on Margaret's face.

'Oh, be careful, your grace!' she exclaimed, as they came very close to another carriage, wishing that the duke would stop looking at her in that very particular way. No wonder the young woman they had just passed had appeared to stare so hard at them.

'W-we are quite safe, Miss L-Lambart,' the duke assured her, turning his attention to the horses once more. 'I promise you, I w-would not upon any account have an accident today.'

'I am delighted to hear it, sir!' Margaret replied in a firm voice, but softening it with a smile.

'I h-had h-hoped that w-we might see my cousin, St George. Selina told me before I set out that she expected him. H-he is not really our cousin, of course, but w-we h-have always seen a good deal of each other, as h-he is my guardian. I kn-know you w-will find h-him exceedingly agreeable, ma'am.'

Margaret looked at the duke a little curiously.

'You admire Lord St George very much, sir?'

'I think h-he is one of the finest men in London, Miss L-Lambart.'

'Then I am sure I shall like his lordship upon your recommendation, your grace.'

'Oh, you w-will like, h-him, Miss L-Lambart, n-no matter what I say!'

thinking his look might be occasioned by genuine concern on his aunt's account, and wishing to set his mind at rest.

'Indeed, ma'am!' Lord St George returned coldly.

'Of course I have not!' Lady James said impatiently. 'I cannot think what your informant can have been about. In fact, as I have mentioned before, I have had a very agreeable time since Miss Lambart arrived. Miss Lambart plays whist quite excellently.'

'I can assure you, from what we heard, dear aunt, we were exceedingly distressed for you!' Lady Selina said. 'I was much upset at not seeing you yesterday.'

'Yes, doubtless that is why David returned alone,' said her aunt drily.

'Alone! What did he want, then?' cried Lady Selina, sharply.

'To see me, of course,' returned her aunt, smiling blandly.

'I — I had to call upon dear Lucy Berrington. She is to give a ball next week, I collect. But she informed me it was to be a very small one — because of her condition, you know — however, I am expecting a card any day now.'

Lady James exchanged a quick glance with Margaret and gave a slight shake of the head. Lord St George noticed this, and an expression of annoyance disturbed his features.

'Well, ma'am, we are glad to know that we have been misinformed,' he said calmly enough. 'Oxford, Selina and I were, of course, worried at the reports we heard. After all, we are among your closest kinsfolk — '

To Margaret's ear he seemed to stress these words; she listened more intently to what Lord St George was saying in an attempt to divine his real meaning.

' — and naturally it was our duty to come to your aid; we are only glad that it is unnecessary.'

Lady Selina looked annoyed in her turn, stared at St George, glanced at Margaret and seemed about to speak, but her aunt said smoothly,

'It is exceedingly kind of you, St George, of you all — to put yourselves out for me, but, as you see, it was quite unnecessary. I am, I think, the very picture of health, and, in any case, I have Miss Lambart at hand to help. I wonder your informant did not mention that she was with me!'

Lady Selina looked extremely cross at this, but Lord St George turned to Margaret.

'I did not gather, I am afraid,' he said in a polite voice, 'quite how long you have been in London, ma'am?'

'It is about four weeks now, sir.'

'And you have been enjoying it?'

'Oh, yes, I thank you, sir. It has been most agreeable.'

'Miss Lambart has found pleasure in driving in the park with Hannah, George!' Lady Selina said with an affected laugh.

'Indeed!' Lord St George's reply was so neutral it was impossible to tell from it what he was thinking. Margaret did not doubt, however, that he must agree with Lady Selina.

'But yesterday, Miss Lambart drove out with David,' Lady James said to the obvious surprise of her nephew and niece. 'He was very glad to have her company,' she finished blandly.

Lord St George raised his eyebrows, and Lady Selina now looked exceedingly angry.

'You have indeed made a hasty conquest, Miss Lambart,' Lord St George observed.

Margaret did not care for his remark, but she smiled politely.

'Hardly that, sir. His grace was so kind as to drive me in the park, but it goes no further, I assure you.'

She was aware that she had not quite succeeded in keeping the tartness out of her voice. She thought she heard Lady Selina say under her breath, 'I should think not indeed!' but when she looked towards her, the girl turned away angrily.

Margaret made a further effort at

polite conversation.

'You have a seat in Oxfordshire, I collect, my lord?'

'That is so, ma'am.'

'My father was at Oxford — at Christ Church College. He always spoke of Oxfordshire as being a very beautiful county, so lush and green. Very like my own Cheshire, I think.'

'I have not visited that side of the Pennines, ma'am.'

'Ah, you know Yorkshire, then?'

'Old John Ford particularly sent his regards to you, ma'am,' Lady Selina cut in. 'All the old servants were asking when they would see you again.'

'You know very well I never venture out of London, my dear Selina. People must come to visit me here. That is why I am particularly glad that Miss Lambart has come to stay in Hanover Square. I have not seen her since she was a small child. Mrs Lambart was one of my dearest friends. We were at school in Reading together.'

'Indeed, I did not know that, ma'am,'

her niece answered with as little show of interest as she dared express.

'Were you at school, Miss Lambart?' Lord St George next asked.

'No, sir, I was educated at home. When I was small there were masters for all that my father could not teach us. And my father had an excellent library, sir; my sisters and I were allowed the run of it.'

'You are fond of reading, then, ma'am?'

'I like particularly histories and biographies, sir. We are lucky to have an excellent subscription library in Burley, our nearest town. And I am very lucky in that Lady James has an exceptional library here.'

'My uncle was something of a collector, ma'am. He was particularly interested in books upon the East.'

'So I have found out, sir. I have passed many agreeable hours browsing among the books here. In fact, I am become quite familiar with some of the later Ming emperors.'

Margaret gave a little smile as she said this, but the marquis did not respond, maintaining his look of polite interest only, while from Lady Selina's corner there came a sound which might have been described as a snort.

'I am very glad to have Miss Lambart taking an interest in your uncle's books,' Lady James said somewhat sharply. '*You* were never one for reading, Selina, except for Mrs Radcliffe or Mrs Parsons, or some fashion journal. And as for you, St George, you have your own libraries which are uncommonly fine, both in London and in Oxfordshire. You have no need of mine.'

The marquis bowed. 'You are very kind, ma'am; I have done my best to add to what was left me; I have considered it my duty.'

'Oh, I am very well aware that you have added to them a great deal, St George; it is one of your less wastefully extravagant occupations. Perhaps Miss Lambart would like to inspect your London books some time. You might ask us to tea, one day.'

The marquis bowed again.

'I should be honoured, ma'am.'

'Then, perhaps, we might be favoured with a glimpse of your Chinese waistcoat, also?'

Lord St George's eyebrows rose. 'Now how on earth, my dear aunt, did you hear about that?'

'Oh, we are not so far out of the world as you imagine, sir, are we, my dear?' Lady James answered airily. 'You would be surprised how much we have been in society of late, and you know very well that involves a quantity of gossip in certain quarters. And you must, of course, expect that people will gossip about you if you will insist on being 'in the pink', as I think you call it.'

The marquis looked at his aunt, clearly somewhat startled. Then he smiled.

'Oh, that sounds like a Mr Anderson, ma'am, if I am not mistaken.'

'You are quite right, sir. We met him at whist the other evening, did not we, my dear?'

'Yes, ma'am.'

'I am surprised to learn that he was there, ma'am,' the marquis now added.

'Oh, Miss Lambart's fame had reached him, and he joined us especially to meet her. Lady Anderson told me that she had been quite pestered by him. He has always declined to oblige her hitherto.'

'Miss Lambart's fame — ?' the marquis queried. 'Pardon me, ma'am, but I do not know to what you are referring.'

'You have been out of London too long, St George,' Lady James returned with an odd little smile. 'You will soon learn, I am sure, that Miss Lambart is a magician at the card table.'

'Indeed!' The marquis turned to survey Margaret, his face quite impassive. 'Then I shall look forward to meeting you there, Miss Lambart. Perhaps you will be kind enough to invite me to your next evening, ma'am.'

Lady Selina had turned round and was listening to this exchange scowling furiously.

'When next I have cards here, I have promised to invite David,' Lady James continued. 'He is quite useless, but he was so anxious to come, I did not like to refuse him. But — the next time, St George, if I am in need of a fourth, I will certainly call upon you.'

The marquis bowed without replying.

'David asked to play cards with you, aunt!' Lady Selina burst out. 'But — he always says you frighten him too much to make the game agreeable!'

'Indeed, Selina! How charmingly you express yourself!'

Lady Selina flushed, and there was a moment's uncomfortable silence.

'I wonder, sir, what you think — ' Margaret began.

'Have you yet had the opportunity to read — ' the marquis started.

Both stopped, and begged the other to proceed.

'I was only about to ask you, sir, how you thought our army in Spain would fare. Will Sir John Moore succeed in passing the Tagus, think you?'

'I have not seen the latest despatches, ma'am. The Times has had nothing new since last week. You are following our fortunes in the field closely, Miss Lambart?'

'As everyone else, sir, I am anxious for victory quickly.'

The marquis surveyed Margaret once more. She thought she could discern a little puzzlement in his countenance as he regarded her.

'My new brother-in-law, Sir Thomas Pettigrew, has something to do with the local volunteers, I collect. He was telling me that there has been a great deal of extra activity in Falmouth; several ships leave there for the Mediterranean every day, he said.'

'Your brother-in-law is Sir Thomas

Pettigrew?' The marquis sounded surprised.

'You know him, sir?' Margaret asked quickly, with a smile.

'I have not had the honour of meeting Sir Thomas himself, but I do know of the family.'

'I think the Pettigrews are a considerable family in Cornwall,' Margaret said quietly.

'You have several sisters, I collect, Miss Lambart?'

'I have four, sir.'

'And they will be missing you very much, I expect. Do you intend making a long stay in London, ma'am?'

'I am not quite certain, sir.' Margaret glanced towards her godmother.

'Miss Lambart will certainly remain with me till the end of the season, St George. After that, we will see. I have hopes of persuading her to stay longer.'

Lady Selina now gave an impatient sigh.

'But Miss Lambart has no expectation

of being received in society, George;' she said now pointedly. 'Miss Lambart particularly mentioned that when David and I met her yesterday.'

The marquis made no answer, but Lady James spoke sharply.

'Miss Lambart may have no such expectation, Selina, but *I* have. I particularly want her to attend everything that a young woman just coming out should attend. I was meaning to ask your advice, St George. You know everybody. Pray, what balls will there be this season?'

'Miss Lambart is only just coming out?' he asked surprised. 'But I had thought — forgive me, ma'am, but I had thought you said Miss Lambart had four sisters all younger than herself, whom she has now safely settled?'

'And so I did, St George; but Miss Lambart has not been in London before, and I wish to give her an agreeable time. I am depending upon you for advice.'

'I will do my best for you, ma'am.'

'St George has a great many calls upon his time, have not you?' Lady Selina now said. 'You live such a secluded life, aunt, I do not think you can know what preparations must go into doing the season. One must, of course, start with the clothes, and there will hardly be time now — '

'Miss Lambart is, I think, already adequately provided with the necessary garments, thank you, Selina. Madame Thérèse already has a ball-gown — '

'Madame Thérèse,' burst out Lady Selina. 'You are taking Miss Lambart to Madame Thérèse?'

Lady James nodded complacently.

'I collect that she is without peer.'

'There, George! What did I tell you!' Lady Selina said angrily, turning to the marquis. 'It is well known that Madame Thérèse is quite the most expensive dress-maker in London, and I hardly think that — '

She stopped abruptly, and stared at Margaret, her glance taking in every detail of her attire.

'Are you suggesting that Miss Lambart ought not to go to Madame Thérèse?' Lady James now enquired icily. 'I would not have thought that was any — '

'Your pardon, ma'am,' the marquis interrupted hastily, 'but I do not think that was Selina's meaning. She was only concerned, I am sure, that through — through insufficient knowledge, Miss Lambart might be led into incurring greater expense than she had anticipated. For someone not experienced in London ways, it would be a very easy mistake to make, and as you yourself have said, ma'am, you have lived somewhat retired from the world and may not be able to advise her for the best.'

'Indeed! Well, let me assure you, St George, we knew perfectly well what we were doing when we bespoke a gown from Madame Thérèse for — for Miss Lambart,' Lady James amended quickly. 'We did not go there blindfold. And now, if you will excuse us, we have other matters to attend to.

Margaret, my dear, will you please ring the bell?'

Unhappily, Margaret did as she was asked. She did not want Lady James to quarrel with her kinsfolk on her account, but really, Lady Selina had been quite insufferable. Margaret wondered why she was so hostile.

And as for the marquis! He was hardly friendly. Privately, Margaret thought he was arrogant and disagreeable, and could not at all see why the young Duke of Oxford was so impressed by him. Certainly, he was very fashionable, but she had seen no pleasant qualities in him. Perhaps they only appeared to people who knew him well, and Margaret felt quite certain that she would never be in that number. Nor had she any wish to be. Doubtless she would have to meet him frequently, as Lady James had said that he was accustomed to visiting her nearly every day when he was in the captial, but perhaps she could manage to be engaged when he came. That would certainly be best. She had no wish for a repetition of this day's encounter.

* * *

The remaining days till the Duchess of Berrington's ball passed without any other incident of note. The Duke of Oxford called upon Margaret every day, and somehow it became the accepted thing that he should conduct her to those sights of London she had not yet seen; she also drove in the park with him upon two further occasions.

On most evenings there were the usual card parties; at the one Lady James herself gave, the duke was also present. He was a no more than adequate player, and was clearly very nervous when he partnered his aunt; but luckily their cards were good, and he escaped with no more than a few tart instructions.

Margaret had wondered rather uncomfortably if the marquis St George would also be present on this occasion,

121

but he did not appear. She knew that he called every day in Hanover Square, because Lady James mentioned the visits, but on no occasion did Margaret meet him. She was glad that the minor breach between the marquis and his aunt had been so quickly healed, and was even more thankful that she did not encounter him. She did him the justice to think he timed his visits very carefully on purpose.

The duke, of course, when he knew that Margaret had met his guardian, was anxious to have her opinion. To please him, Margaret commented favourably on the marquis's appearance, but more than that she could not do. She was quite unable to enter into the young man's enthusiasm, and so maintained a judicious silence, and as soon as she could she turned the conversation into other channels.

When the day of the ball at last arrived, to her surprise Margaret found herself looking forward to it a great deal more than she had expected. She had not danced in public for many years, but she had participated in impromptu country dances, and so, though she was not in doubt about her ability to acquit herself with sufficient credit, she had no great confidence that she would have many partners. Lady James had urged her not to mention that they had received cards for the duchess's ball, but she supposed his Grace of Oxford might be there, and that she could depend upon him for at least one pair of dances. And then, surely her hostess would see to it that she did not sit out the entire evening! Margaret determined to enjoy herself whatever happened.

As she was going upstairs to dress, Lady James summoned her into her boudoir.

'Margaret, my dear,' her godmother began, and then stopped, looking somewhat embarrassed.

'Yes, ma'am?'

'I — er — I hope you will forgive me, and I beg you not to wear them

if you do not like them, but — er — '
Lady James paused again.

'Wear what, ma'am?' Margaret asked,
very puzzled.

'Margaret, my dear,' the older woman
began again, 'I know you do not
possess any jewellery of your own.
You told me that you had had to
sell all your dear mother's — but, this
evening, I think we shall see women
wearing some of the most valuable
gems in London. I have no wish to
offend you, my dear, but I would
like to offer you the loan of some
of my pieces. They are kept hidden
away now, for I have no use for them,
but I have had what I think are the
most suitable pieces brought from my
jewellers — '

Lady James stopped, looking exceedingly pink, and she gestured towards a
heavy leather box which was open on
a chest. In the box Margaret could
see several old-fashioned pieces, the
stones of which appeared to be, to
her inexpert eyes, of first quality.

Margaret was very touched. 'Oh, ma'am!' she cried. 'You are so kind. They are the most beautiful jewels I have ever seen! But — I should be a great deal too frightened to wear them. I should be worried all the time that I might lose something. You see, I have never had anything so valuable in my possession before!'

'It — it would give me a great deal of pleasure if you would wear something, my dear,' Lady James said quite timidly. 'I know that they are not quite in the latest mode, and that some young women would not wear them on that account, but I am sure you will not bother with that. It is a great shame that they should always be locked up now; they were once very much admired!'

'I am sure they were!' Margaret cried. 'They are magnificent!'

'So, please choose what you like, my dear,' her godmother went on, nodding and smiling.

Margaret looked into the box, and

held the pieces up in turn. Finally she picked out two pieces which looked the least flamboyant; a pearl necklace with a small diamond drop, and a pretty little tiara of pearls formed as flowers with diamond centres and leaves.

'I think perhaps these would suit me best, ma'am. Besides, my dress would not show off these brighter stones.'

'An excellent choice, Margaret, but you must have earrings also. Perhaps those I wore the other evening would do — the pearl drops with the diamond bows.'

'I have never worn anything so costly, ma'am,' said Margaret fingering the tiara.

'You are not to think about that, my dear. You are to wear them and enjoy them. And I shall like to see you in them. They are very suitable for you. Besides, they match your name.'

Margaret bent down and kissed her godmother's cheek.

'You are so kind to me, ma'am. It

126

is far more than I have any right to expect.'

'Nonsense, my dear! And I may say I am looking forward to this evening a very great deal myself. Because of — of Caroline,' and here, for a moment, Lady James went pink, then continued briskly, 'well, I have not had the pleasure of bringing out anyone before. I am looking forward to seeing my charge admired and envied.'

'Oh, ma'am,' Margaret said, smiling, but much moved, 'you must not wait about for me; you must go to the card-room as soon as you may in order to get a good table.'

'I shall probably go to play sometime during the evening, but first I mean to sit on a sofa in the dowagers' corner — as you tell me *you* have done so often — and discuss this season's crop of young ladies. That is a pleasure I have so far been denied; my nieces had no need of me to bring them out, so you must not grudge me the delight now. Besides, you would not deprive me of the compliments I am to receive!'

'Oh, ma'am, I am afraid you have little hope of many such!' Margaret laughed. 'You should have picked on someone much younger to bring out if you have a taste for them.'

'Now, listen to me, my dear. You must not forever keep reminding people that you are — that you are not in the first blush of youth. You do not look within years of your true age now, and people will only think that perhaps you were in mourning when you should have made your debut. Besides, when you are presented, I have no doubt that there will be a great many women older than you: brides and — and others — '

'Presented, ma'am! Me!' Margaret exclaimed.

'But of course, my dear; it is usual.'

'But — but — '

'We have not time to discuss it now, my dear. Do you go and dress now; I am longing to see you when you are ready. Rely upon Hannah's advice. She has impeccable taste and will be upon her mettle tonight. I have complete confidence in her judgement where matters of dress are concerned.'

And when Margaret reappeared in Lady James's boudoir some time later, it was abundantly clear that her ladyship's confidence was not misplaced.

The drive to Berrington House did not take long, and they found quite a crowd outside waiting to quiz the arrivals. A carpet had been laid on the pavement, the house blazed with light at every window, and sounds of music drifted out into the street. If the usually sedate Margaret had felt some excitement before, it was increased a hundredfold now. They went first to the cloakroom to remove their shawls, and there Lady James found herself party to many astonished reunions. Margaret, of course, was presented to these long-unseen acquaintances and met their daughters, so that by the time they were ready to ascend to the ballroom she knew at least a dozen ladies to whom she could nod later in the evening. She received several congratulations upon her appearance, and caught several covert glances at the jewels she was wearing.

For someone accustomed to being considered excessively dowdy, not to say frumpish, this was heady wine indeed, and the praise brought an unaccustomed bloom to Margaret's cheek. As she took a last look at herself in the glass, it seemed almost a stranger who looked gravely back at her. She saw a simple white dress with a train edged with gold embroidery and pearls which Madame Thérèse had contrived to fit her to perfection, and which had cost a sum which had made Margaret shudder when she knew it. Lady James, of course, had paid for the dress for it was quite beyond Margaret's means, but Margaret had insisted on paying for the fan she needed to match the dress, and that little lace and ivory gewgaw had cost her the remainder of the money she had brought with her from Cheshire.

She had felt quite wicked when she first contemplated spending so much on a mere fan, but she succumbed, as she knew she must, to Hannah's remark that 'it would not do to let her ladyship down in the matter of her dress', and so she had shut her eyes to the price metaphorically, and had ordered the fan, silently determining not to spend a single penny more upon clothes, no matter what the function was to which she was invited.

Now she looked again at the pearls and diamonds in their old-fashioned settings which adorned her neck and her hair and her ears, and she was quite unable to repress an unaccustomed little thrill of pride. Old-fashioned the settings might be, borrowed the jewels might be, but so far she had not seen any woman wearing finer, or more beautiful gems.

They walked side by side up the red-carpeted steps to the ballroom with liveried flunkeys on either side, and for a moment Margaret felt as nervous as any young girl attending her very first ball. But a vision of her sisters' astonished exclamations if they could see her quickly restored her control, and when she was at last standing before her hostess, she was once more her usual calm self.

The welcome the duchess extended to them both was warm, and she took hold of Margaret's hand.

'Dear Miss Lambart, I was so afraid something would happen to prevent you coming tonight. Berrington has made me rest indoors all this week, except for a strict half hour's drive each day, but if you had not come this evening, I should have insisted upon waiting upon you tomorrow; I have so wanted to see you again — to thank you myself for all your kindness.'

'It was what anyone would have done, your grace!' protested Margaret.

But the duchess shook her head.

'I did not notice the rush to help

when you were trying to get me to that sofa! But we must talk again later. It is so kind of you to come to our little ball. To tell you the truth,' the duchess went on, whispering close to Margaret's ear, 'we have had to invite rather more couples than we had intended at first, for it seemed that we might otherwise offend too many if we kept it too exclusive. Not that I care a jot for that, but I must consider Berrington's position in the government. Still, it will not compete with the balls which are to be held later in the season, I am sure. Berrington wishes to remain in London only for this month, but I shall try to bargain for at least mid-July.' And she smiled delightfully at Margaret.

The duke was equally cordial, exclaiming once again over the coincidence of Margaret's being Lady James's god-daughter, and that it should have been she who was behind the duchess at the crucial moment in the art gallery, and he was prepared to say a great deal more in the way of thanks and appreciation, but for the fact that the next guests were waiting to be greeted.

No sooner had they moved forward into the ballroom than Margaret saw Lord St George hurrying towards them. He was the last person she would have wished to see so very early in the evening, but she braced herself to be polite.

The marquis bent over his aunt's hand and bowed to Margaret.

'I had no idea that I should have the pleasure of seeing you here this evening, dear aunt. I am sure that you had not mentioned receiving the duchess's cards. I did not know that you were acquainted with her.'

'I saw no reason to tell you, St George,' Lady James returned, a shade of tartness in her voice.

The marquis smiled, almost indulgently.

'Ah, ma'am, and I was quite under the impression that I had been forgiven.'

'I told you that I would endeavour to overlook what you had said, but, certainly, I promised no more.'

'I can only apologise most humbly once more, then, ma'am. I beg you to remember that I spoke with what I considered your own best interests at heart.'

'Well, sir,' Lady James returned, with a quick glance at Margaret, 'I would point out that this evening you are in some position to make amends.'

The marquis inclined his head to his aunt, then turned to Margaret. His eyes narrowed slightly as he looked at her, but his voice betrayed nothing as he spoke to her with formal politeness.

'Permit me to say, Miss Lambart, that you are looking exceedingly charming.'

'You are very kind, sir.'

Lady James looked very pleased at this small exchange, and gave Margaret an 'I told you so' glance.

Margaret had not at first intended to say anything more, but a little devil suddenly prodded her to add,

'But I think you must be dazzled by the jewels, my lord. Lady James was so kind as to lend them to me as I have none of my own. She did not like to think that I should be under-dressed in such a very fashionable company.'

She smiled innocently at the marquis, and he gave her a sharp look. He might have said something, but Lady James was already expostulating.

'Now there is no need for you to have told St George that, my dear. It is none of his business. Besides, as you know, I like to have things used, rather than always shut away. And these pieces have not been used for long enough.'

'But when I receive such compliments, ma'am,' Margaret said with a smile as she remembered how Lady James had almost forced her nephew to make the compliment, 'I feel I receive them under false pretences, and I am constrained to account for the effect achieved with borrowed plumes.'

'You are too honest, my dear. I hope you will not return the same answer when other compliments come your way this evening, as they assuredly will, will not they, St George?'

'Oh, assuredly, ma'am! Miss Lambart looks quite magnificent, and I was not referring to the jewels,' he added in a lower voice so that only Margaret could hear the words.

Margaret looked at him quickly, not at all sure whether he was speaking genuinely or not. She met his eyes for a moment, but then he turned again to his aunt, and Margaret found her speculation on this cut short by the rapid approach of two figures.

'My dear aunt!' Lady Selina cried, 'we had no idea that you were to be here. You did not mention receiving the duchess's card. I did not know you were acquainted, and in any case, believed that you had given up balls entirely!'

'*I* did not receive the duchess's card, Selina,' Lady James returned tartly. '*I* am here entirely on account of Miss Lambart. It is *she* to whom the cards were sent.'

Lady Selina stared. 'But — '

'I was, of course,' Lady James continued smoothly, 'a friend of the late duchess, Berrington's mother, but I do not recollect meeting the present duchess before, though I am, of course, acquainted with her family. Oh no, you quite mistake; I am here under Miss Lambart's auspices — '

'Oh, no, ma'am! Your pardon, but that is not the case at all!' Margaret protested.

'Indeed it is!' Lady James said with a rather severe look. 'I know what regard you have for the truth, my dear, and I have no wish to make my appearance this evening under false pretences. David, dear boy, how are you?'

The duke kissed his aunt's hand and bowed to Margaret.

'Miss L-Lambart, if you are n-not otherwise engaged, may I h-have the honour of the first dance with you?'

'Thank you, sir,' Margaret said simply, and the duke offered her his arm. She put her hand on it, and, excusing themselves to the others the duke led her on to the floor where they were making up the first quadrille. Margaret was very conscious of the stares of two pairs of eyes as they walked away.

'I-I did not h-hope to see you h-here tonight, Miss L-Lambart, but I suppose the Berringtons are old f-friends?'

Margaret was very well aware that the duke was not trying to probe in any impertinent manner as his sister might have done, so she answered straightforwardly,

'Oh, no, sir. I have been acquainted with the duchess but a few days.'

'And yet — you were invited — !' The duke was quite plainly astonished, and then, realising how his exclamation must have sounded, blushed very red and cried, 'Oh, I beg your pardon, Miss L-Lambart, I-I did n-not mean — '

Margaret smiled and put her hand upon his arm. 'I know you did not, sir, and the circumstances which brought my invitation were, to tell you the truth, quite exceptional.'

The dance began then, and Margaret and the duke spoke but little for a time. But he often smiled at her, and Margaret noticed that when he was not called upon to talk, he was a good deal less afflicted by blushing. He was, she observed, as he stood opposite her, a very pleasant-looking young man. When he had acquired rather more assurance and the youthful outlines of his face had matured, he could well become an extremely handsome one.

The dancing was a great pleasure; she had done little enough of it in recent years, but Margaret had not lost her natural grace of movement, and she performed all the figures of the dance with pleasure and confidence.

The duke said with his customary blush, 'You dance so well, Miss L-Lambart; there must be some excellent teachers in Cheshire.'

'I thank you, sir, but you forget how many years of practice I have had,'

Margaret answered with a smile.

The duke frowned at this.

'You must forgive me if I speak p-plainly, Miss L-Lambart, but I do n-not n-notice that that may be the case till you remind me of the possibility, which, I must say, you do v-very frequently.' He looked straight at her then, his whole face quite scarlet, but his eyes very earnest. Then he looked down. 'Your pardon, ma'am,' he murmured. 'I h-have spoken too freely; I h-have no right.'

'Oh, pray do not think of it, sir,' Margaret said quickly, laying her hand upon his arm; 'you have not offended me at all. I would not dream of letting a matter of no account like that upset me. Indeed, I think it quite right that there should be plain speaking between friends. And I hope I may think that we are friends?'

The duke looked up, his face wreathed in smiles. He clutched Margaret's hand in both of his.

'Oh, Miss L-Lambart, I should l-like

that of all things! To be your friend!'

'That is agreed, then,' said Margaret, returning his broad smile as she looked up at him. 'But — I think we are hindering the dance somewhat.'

And Margaret withdrew her hand and stepped backward. The duke continued to gaze at her with shining eyes, and was not at all prepared for the next movement of the dance.

At the conclusion of the first two dances, the duke took Margaret back to Lady James, who was in conversation with the duke of Berrington. When Margaret sat down, the latter bowed to her and said, 'I am come to solicit the next dances, Miss Lambart. I trust that you are not already engaged?'

'No, indeed, sir, I thank you. As I know almost nobody here, I do not expect to be much in demand!'

'Then I shall certainly see to it that your expectations come to nought, Miss Lambart,' Berrington replied. 'The duchess would be exceedingly annoyed with me if she found that you, of all people, were sitting out any of the dances at her ball. I am also commissioned by her to request that you and Lady James will be so kind as to join our table for supper'.

'You are very kind, sir.'

'Then, if you will forgive me, ma'am,' he said bowing to Lady James and Margaret, and with another to the young duke, 'I will go and speak to some of our other guests. But — we are engaged for the second dances, Miss Lambart.' And he looked at Margaret with a friendly smile.

'Yes, sir,' she replied, 'I promise I shall not forget!'

Then she turned to Lady James.

'Do not you wish to join the card tables, ma'am? I shall be able to find my way there to you.'

'Yes, yes, my dear, I shall go to play shortly. But I confess I have been enjoying watching the dance. You and David looked very well together.'

The duke blushed with pleasure, and then they were joined by Lady Selina and Lord St George. Lady Selina sat down on the other side of Lady James.

'Did ever you see such a number of old friends, ma'am? How very agreeable this is after the crushes we have known. I suppose you are not acquainted with many persons here, Miss Lambart,' she suddenly said to Margaret, speaking across her aunt. 'You will realize, of course, that only the very highest of the ton have been invited.'

'Indeed!' Margaret returned calmly. 'I am afraid I am so ignorant of London society, ma'am, that I had not realised the case. I collect I should consider myself extremely lucky to be here!'

Lady Selina did not answer, but from her expression it was clear that Margaret had voiced her opinion exactly. Lady James murmured a shocked, 'My dear!' and Margaret looked across at Lady Selina blandly. Suddenly a frown crossed Lady Selina's face. She stared at Margaret sharply, her eyes moving from the necklace about Margaret's throat to the tiara in her shining brown hair.

'But surely — ' she cried, ' — those are the — !' She stopped abruptly, looked first at her aunt, then at Lord St George, then back to the necklace.

For the first time that evening, Margaret felt annoyed. Really, this girl's impertinence seemed boundless!

'Selina!' Lady James said angrily.

Margaret maintained her smile, but her eyes were hard.

'Yes, you are quite right to recognize the jewels, Lady Selina,' she said lightly. 'Lady James was so kind as to lend me some of hers as I have none of my own to wear for this evening.'

Lady James, her mouth a tight line, and her face quite flushed, said firmly, 'Miss Lambart was so kind as to agree to wear some of my old-fashioned pieces. I was extremely glad to have them in use again. Pearls are always the better for being worn. They weep, you know, if shut up too long.'

'But *I* would always be glad to wear

them for you, dearest aunt!' Lady Selina cried. 'After all, they only need resetting to be the very finest — '

'I do not care to have them reset, miss!' Lady James retorted; 'and I remember quite clearly your telling me once that it would be utter purgatory — I am sure that was your phrase — utter purgatory to you to appear in anything not absolutely in the latest fashion. In any case, pearls would not suit you; your colouring is far too insipid for them. They need someone with the stronger colouring of Miss Lambart's complexion. Her skin makes them glow. On you, they would look nothing. Besides, pearls are particularly suited to Miss Lambart because of her name, Margaret. Miss Lambart has been a pearl to me. I have had more pleasure since she has been in Hanover Square than I have had in years. I am finding it very agreeable to have a young person about the house, and I am hoping Miss Lambart will agree to spend a great deal of time with me.' Lady James looked round challengingly at two members of her family.

Lady Selina sat back pouting. Margaret thought she heard the exclamation 'Young!' under her breath, and the pause after Lady James finished speaking threatened to become an awkward one. But Lord St George now bowed to Margaret.

'I had been hoping to secure your hand for the next dances, Miss Lambart, if you are not engaged?' he said quietly.

Margaret was very glad to be able to reply as she did.

'Thank you, sir, but I regret I have already promised the next pair.'

The marquis looked rather surprised, and glanced questioningly at the young duke who was looking exceedingly flushed and unhappy. The young man saw his guardian's look and was about to disclaim the honour when Lady Selina exclaimed in a pleased voice, 'Oh look! There is our host, and I do believe he is coming this way!'

5

The Duke of Berrington was indeed approaching them, and when he had not yet reached them Lady Selina gave a simpering smile, and declared in her rather high voice, 'Such a delightful evening, your Grace. I have never seen your ballroom to more advantage. The flowers are too lovely!'

'Thank you, ma'am,' the duke said civilly, 'you are very kind. Good evening to you again, St George. I wondered what had become of you. I believe our glass houses at Oaxborough are quite denuded for this evening, Lady Selina.'

'Ah, you have always such variety there. I am always telling my brother Oxford that he should seek your advice on his planting. We never seem to have near enough blooms for anything when they are needed! It is exceedingly disagreeable to be so curtailed when one wishes to provide a particular effect, but of course I am never listened to!'

'Did I hear that you have been to see Downton, Oxford?' the older man said, turning to the young duke with a smile. 'You certainly could not do better than to follow his advice.'

Oxford started to speak, but Lady Selina interrupted him with another dazzling smile at her host.

'Such delightful music you have also, your Grace! I quite dote upon these tunes. They positively make one's feet tap to keep the time!'

'I am delighted that you approve them, ma'am. But now, if you will excuse me, I think they are waiting to start the next dance.'

And bowing generally, the duke offered his arm to Margaret.

'This is our dance, Miss Lambart, I think.'

Margaret rose, excused herself to the others, took the duke's proferred arm, and was led to the top of the first set. Once more she was aware of eyes boring into her back.

The duke was a most agreeable partner, and chatted lightly whenever they had to await their turn. When he learnt that she had four sisters all married, he was all congratulations.

'There are not many mothers in London society who could claim as much, ma'am!'

'Ah, but the higher one goes in society, sir, the smaller the choice naturally is. At our level, the field is really quite wide; it is just a matter of putting a young woman in the way of eligible men! But there are not, I fancy, a great many eligible dukes in London society!'

The duke laughed. 'You make it sound a great deal easier, Miss Lambart, than I am sure it is! Surely it is necessary for the young women to be agreeable, and pretty, too, if it is possible! Though little can be done about the latter, I fear, the former reflects a great deal on those who have had charge of their upbringing. And when you tell me that the dowries were not so substantial, your achievement is all the more remarkable, ma'am! I salute you.'

'Pray sir, continue,' Margaret said gaily. 'I have not been used to flattery such as this, and I find it remarkably agreeable!'

'I assure you, ma'am, it is no flattery! I am greatly admiring indeed. And not only I! Have not you seen how many eyes there are upon us? You cannot be unconscious of them!'

'It is no wonder, sir, that people should look astonished, for here am I, an unknown creature of advanced years, dancing the second dances with his Grace of Berrington! What should they do but stare?'

'I will not accept all you say,' the duke laughed. 'Your advanced years indeed! And unknown! As for that, even I have heard the remarkable feats you have performed at the card-table!'

Margaret looked as she felt surprised. 'But I have only played in the small parties attended by Lady James!'

'You forget, Miss Lambart, men gossip a very great deal in their clubs!'

The dances were over, and the duke led Margaret from the floor. Lady James was no longer in her place, and so the duke conducted Margaret to the card-room. On the way there, they approached a man neatly dressed in black, but for his plain gilt buttons, and his white shirt. His face was extraordinarily highly-complexioned, and his brown hair was dressed close to his head.

'Ah, Brummell, so you are come!' exclaimed the duke, shaking the man's hand. Then he turned to Margaret. 'Miss Lambart, may I present Major George Brummell of the Belvoir Volunteers. This is Miss Lambart from Cheshire, Brummell. She has lately arrived in London.'

Major Brummell bowed and Margaret curtseyed. She looked at the newcomer with a good deal of interest, for the loquacious Mr Anderson had confided to her once that society was in awe of him. He certainly did not look at all frightening now.

'I hope you are enjoying your visit to London, ma'am,' she heard him saying.

'Oh, I am indeed, sir! Everyone has been so kind.'

'Kind!' exclaimed Major Brummell, 'you surprise me exceedingly, ma'am. I should not have thought that London society was notable for its kindness. I shall be very glad to hear of it. What evidence have you for saying it?' He turned to the duke. 'You may safely leave Miss Lambart with me, Berrington. Clearly, she has such a good-natured view of Society, I shall not dare to spoil it.'

'Miss Lambart and I are on our way to the card-room. Miss Lambart is here with her god-mother, the Lady James Feniton, and Lady James is now doubtless deep in whist.'

'Then *I* will conduct Miss Lambart. I confess that I am now more curious than ever. I had not thought Lady James ventured out any more, but Miss Lambart has achieved a second miracle. In addition to thinking London society *kind* — '

'I will not have you making game of Miss Lambart, Brummell,' the duke said firmly. 'If that is to be the case — '

'No, no! I am quite convinced Miss Lambart and I shall agree very well. If you will allow me, ma'am,' and he held out his arm to Margaret.

With a smile, she took it.

'There, you see,' said Major Brummell. 'Now, you look to your other guests, Berrington, and leave Miss Lambart to me. I can see that she is a creature of excellent good sense — and great taste.'

Margaret had caught her cavalier take a quick look at her jewels. She was certain that in that short glance he had appraised them to a nicety.

The duke excused himself with a

smile, and Major Brummell said, 'Do you prefer to walk, ma'am, to sit out, or would you like to join me in the next dance?'

'I should like to dance, sir, if that is agreeable to you. But first, I think I should let Lady James know where I am.'

'Very well. Tell me, ma'am,' he said as they walked, 'how comes it that you have not before visited your — godmother, Lady James?'

'Oh, that is easily explained. I am the eldest of five sisters, sir. When we were orphaned, of course I had to look after them; but, I am happy to say that the youngest was married last April.'

'The others are all married also?'

Margaret nodded.

'Ah. So now you are free to enjoy yourself?'

'Precisely, sir,' Margaret answered with a smile.

The Major smiled back. They found Lady James and Margaret presented Major Brummell to her. Very formally, he requested Lady James's permission to lead her god-daughter out for the next dance. This was given, and Margaret and her partner then made their way back to the ballroom.

She could not but be aware of the sensation their appearance caused. Major Brummell progressed forward with Margaret on his arm, occasionally nodding to acquaintances. He led her to the first set and installed them both at the top.

When they were waiting for the music to begin, a man came up behind Major Brummell, clearly enquiring who Margaret was.

'What!' exclaimed Mr Brummell. 'Do not you know Miss Lambart from Cheshire? One of *the* Lambarts of Cheshire. You surprise me exceedingly, sir. Everybody who *is* anybody is acquainted with Miss Lambart. Oh, no, dear boy, I cannot possibly present you. Our dance is to begin. Pray excuse me.'

And Major Brummell offered Margaret

his hand, and they embarked on the first set.

'Major Brummell,' Margaret admonished with a laugh when they were at rest again, 'I could not help but hear what you were saying to your friend.'

'Yes, ma'am?' he said.

'One of *the* Lambarts of Cheshire!' She could not help laughing.

'I do not know what you mean, ma'am!'

'My family are just — Lambarts, not *the* Lambarts, sir!'

'Well, ma'am, I did not say anything incorrect, I think!' he said seriously, but his eyes were twinkling. 'You are one of the Lambarts of Cheshire, are not you? I was sure the duke had said that; did I mistake? Are there Lambarts apart from your family?'

'I do not think so, sir.'

'There we are then! Now, what else did I say to that importunate creature? Oh, yes! That anyone who *was* anyone was acquainted with you. Well, *I* am acquainted with you, so there again I spoke the absolute truth. I really feel it very unkind in you, Miss Lambart, to accuse me of dishonesty!'

'Indeed, sir!' cried Margaret laughing. 'I meant no such thing! But though I rebut the charge of dishonesty, I am right to protest at your innuendo. You make me sound like a great lady, and that I am very far from — '

'You *are* a great lady, ma'am,' interrupted the Major. 'Indeed, at the moment you are the *greatest* lady here, Miss Lambart, for you are now dancing with *me*. If I decide to dance again after our dances, I am afraid you will be demoted. If, however, I do not dance again, then you will remain the greatest lady here this evening.'

'In that case, sir, I suppose I must wish that you have a sudden access of gout, for it would do my consequence no good to be so put down!'

'Miss Lambart, I beg you, wish no such thing! There is no need to be so drastic. Adorned as you are, I see no one else with whom I might care to dance, so your consequence is safe without recourse to inferior or superior powers! May I congratulate you upon your jewels? They are quite some of the finest I have seen. I wonder that they have not been seen before in London.'

'Oh, but — ' Margaret began, then remembered her godmother's words: 'There is no need to tell anyone that the jewels are not yours, my dear.' She decided to follow her instinctive course.

'Yes, they *are* very beautiful, are not they, Major Brummell? My godmother, Lady James, was so kind as to lend them to me as I have none of my own.'

Major Brummell looked at her a little oddly for a moment, then he said with a slight bow, 'It is you who add lustre to the jewels, Miss Lambart; they add nothing to you.'

To her astonished embarrassment, Margaret felt herself blushing like a girl of seventeen.

'You are very kind, sir,' she managed

to utter in nearly her normal voice.

After their pair of dances, her partner offered Margaret his arm.

'I find it very warm in here, ma'am,' he said. 'Would you care for some wine?'

'It is a little warm. Thank you. It would be very pleasant.'

'Have you seen the Berringtons' gallery, yet, ma'am?'

'No, sir.'

'They have a famous collection of paintings. It is reckoned one of the sights of London. It is very agreeable to sit there.'

Major Brummell led her to a higher floor which was, in effect, a long gallery, divided into small areas by pillars and draped curtains making a series of alcoves. He settled Margaret on a sofa some way down in front of a painting of an Italian landscape, which he declared was the prize of the collection.

'I am hiding you here, Miss Lambart, so that no one will discover you before

I return. You are quite screened by this curtain, and I shall not be more than a few minutes, I promise you. You may contemplate the glories of Tuscany while I am gone. I hope we shall have a very interesting conversation when I return.'

With that, Major Brummell disappeared, and Margaret leaned back to gaze at and enjoy the picture before her.

She had only been there a few moments when she heard a woman's voice and the sound of steps on the stairs. They were too far away for Margaret to distinguish the words, but she felt rather sorry that she and Major Brummell would not have undisturbed possession of the gallery. The voice became clearer as its owner drew nearer.

' — but you must see it! It is all too plain! She has already wormed her way into my aunt's confidence — if not her affections! And to what purpose? That, too, is plain! She expects my aunt to leave her her fortune! Heaven knows, she has nothing of her own!'

'She has never pretended otherwise, I think,' Margaret heard Lord St George's voice say next.

'Did not you think it brazen the way she appeared in my aunt's jewels? You know very well those pieces are from the Hellington parure!'

'I have never seen the set, Selina. Have you?'

'No. But what is that to the purpose? It is known that they are the most famous river pearls in England.'

'I thought they suited Miss Lambart perfectly,' Lord St George observed.

'To say that *my* complexion was too — insipid for them!' Lady Selina snapped. 'Had I a brother of any use at all I might have looked to him to protect me from such impertinence. But, oh, no! He is so besotted by the creature already, he is quite unable to do his duty by me! Do you see how he looks at her? Like a — a moon-calf! But, then, David has always been stupid. He cannot see what she is about! She aims to be a duchess yet! And she — near old enough to be his mother!'

Margaret sat frozen to her seat, not daring to move. She had, immediately she had recognized the voices, meant to make her presence known, but before she could do so, she had heard enough to know the subject of their talk. Now she could not decide whether it would be better to remain hidden, hoping that they would go, and thus embarrassing no one but herself, or whether she should reveal herself, thus risking either the embarrassment of all three, or, if Lady Selina were too incensed, the possibility of a public brawl. While she was agitatedly trying to make up her mind how to proceed, she heard St George's voice again.

'You are too harsh on her, Selina. I do not think she has any such plan — '

'Of course she has! It is plain to see! From the first moment she set eyes on

Oxford, she was smiling at him,' Lady Selina interrupted sharply.

'Nor do I think she is trying to wheedle money or jewels out of our aunt,' Lord St George continued firmly. 'But I am somewhat concerned for my aunt herself. After all, we know nothing of this Miss Lambart. She may be using our aunt as her introduction to society which she would not otherwise — '

'Yes,' spat out Lady Selina viciously. 'All that nonsense about the cards being sent to Miss Lambart! How could that creature possibly know dear Lucy Berrington well enough to receive them?'

'And I am concerned that my aunt is not hurt,' went on Lord St George as if his cousin had not spoken. 'She is a very generous old lady, who has been out of the world so long she perhaps has forgotten that there may be adventuresses about. I do not care to think my aunt is being made use of. I do not say that that *is* Miss Lambart's purpose, but I certainly intend to watch her. My aunt is clearly much attached to her already.'

'I cannot think why,' came Lady Selina's voice fretfully. 'She is certainly nothing to look at, and her manners are exceedingly provincial! Why, do you know, she even offered me refreshment when I called upon my aunt — *me* — refreshment! And she has no sense of dress — her gown this evening leaves a great deal to be desired. And as for her manners! They are a great deal too forward! Did you see how she forced Berrington to dance with her?'

'*I* thought our host was very happy to dance with her.'

'Of course he was not! In any case, he should have led *me* out first — !'

An icy voice cut across Lady Selina's. 'Excuse me, madam.'

Suddenly, hot with shame, Margaret heard Major Brummell's voice.

'Oh, Mr Brummell!' Lady Selina gushed. 'How very delightful to see you again! I did not know that you were already returned to London. I

165

hope we shall have the pleasure of seeing you soon in Berkeley Street.'

There was a pause. Then the icy voice came again.

'That is hardly likely. Excuse me, St George.'

Margaret heard Lady Selina cry, 'But Mr Brummell!' and in a moment the Major was standing beside her, bearing two glasses of wine.

'Miss Lambart,' he said in rather a loud voice, and with a slight bow, 'I hope this is to your taste.'

Margaret took one glass with a quivering smile.

'Thank you, sir,' she managed to whisper.

Gratefully she bent her head and tasted the wine. She knew not what to do. Shame and embarrassment alternated with anger and misery. That she should be thought of as — an adventuress! Never had she felt so shamed. She had never thought — not for one moment — but — such suspicions would account for the hostility

— and the rudeness — she had been shown by the marquis and Lady Selina. Certainly, the marquis had not appeared to think she was as black as did the lady — but — worried for his aunt's sake! Oh, it was too much! For several awful moments she feared that she would not be able to control her tears, but would dissolve in weeping such as she had not experienced for many years.

'You will permit me, ma'am,' she heard Major Brummell ask, but before she had replied, he had sat down beside her.

She felt him watching her for a moment, then he pulled out his kerchief, which Margaret even at that moment, noticed was spotless and dazzling as was all his linen, and handed it to her.

'Come, Miss Lambart,' he said in a kind and gentle voice, 'blow your nose! It will make you feel a good deal better!'

She managed to give him another

quavering smile, then set down her glass, took the proferred kerchief, and did as she was bid.

'There,' he said, 'now, do not you feel that things are not so bad after all? It is wonderful, I always think, what a certain amount of physical exertion will accomplish.'

'I can remember giving exactly this advice to my sisters, sir,' Margaret whispered in a tremulous voice. 'I had not thought ever to be in need of it myself again!'

'Well now,' he went on, handing her her glass once more, 'take a good sip of wine; it will steady you amazingly. If there is one thing I must say for Berrington,' he said in his normal, languid tones, 'it is that you may depend upon having very palatable wine at his receptions.' He drank a little wine himself, and then continued pleasantly, 'Doubtless you will now have changed your opinion of London society, Miss Lambart. It is not, you see, all so magnanimous as you had given me to think. As you know, I had thought you mistaken, but rather hoped I might be proved wrong. However — !'

'Oh, Major Brummell!' Margaret whispered, still not daring to look up. 'I am very sorry that you should have overheard — '

'While I, on the contrary, ma'am, am exceedingly glad I returned when I did. It is a matter which, I am happy to say, I can do something to rectify.'

'Oh, pray do nothing, Major Brummell! I beg you. Please forget that you overheard anything! It was not meant for you!'

'Nor for you, ma'am, I think.'

Margaret shook her head miserably. 'I — I should have — let them know that I was here! Only — I hoped to avoid a scene! I thought that if — that if they did not know — ' Margaret was near to tears.

'I am sorry that you have been so wounded, Miss Lambart. I hold myself in part responsible, as it was I who brought you here.'

'Oh, no, sir! If I had not been so pusillanimous — '

'You acted as a lady, Miss Lambart. I do not pretend to understand the cause of what I heard, though I may guess, but I did not care for the phrases I did hear.' Major Brummell sounded very determined.

'But — if you consider it from — from their point of view, sir, it is, I think, understandable! I mean — I am not *anybody*, in spite of what you were kind enough to say.' Margaret managed to look into Major Brummell's face with a rather tremulous smile at this. 'I arrived in London and came to stay in my godmother's house, and none of her kinsfolk knew anything about me! Probably they had never heard of me! Then I appear at this ball in jewels borrowed from her, and — it is not difficult to guess their feelings! I might feel the same, were I in their shoes!'

'You would never have such ignoble thoughts, Miss Lambart,' said Major Brummell firmly. 'And now drink up your wine. It is time for us to take a little promenade.'

'How do you mean, sir?'

'We are going to walk through the rooms together, Miss Lambart, and I am going to see who is fit to be presented to you. If you would do me the honour of allowing me to accompany you?'

'You are very kind, Major Brummell. Mr Anderson told me what a kind person you were — '

'Mr Anderson? And who, pray, is Mr Anderson?'

'Mr Robert Anderson. I believe he is the nephew of Lady Anderson. I met him at cards one evening.'

'Oh. Mr *Robert* Anderson. Yes, I recollect him now. His dress is much improved of late, I notice.'

'He has, I know, modelled himself upon you, sir.'

'He could not do better. I wonder why he told you I was kind. No, do not say anything, Miss Lambart. I have no wish to be disillusioned again. So you have Mr Anderson for an acquaintance. Now, what others have you?'

Margaret named some of the people she had met at cards. Major Brummell listened in silence.

'They hardly sound exciting, ma'am,' he commented when she had finished. 'Well, we will see who there is here whom it would be a pleasure for you to know.'

And they descended to the reception rooms once more. There Major Brummell looked about the company through his glass, and when he had quizzed them all, he proceeded to introduce Margaret to some half a dozen people: two dowagers, one younger woman of her own age, and three very handsome and gentlemanly-looking men, all six of whom bore titles of great distinction and age.

At one point they passed near Lady Selina. She smiled at Major Brummell rather tentatively, Margaret noticed, but the Major took absolutely no notice, and looking through her as though she had not existed, he nodded affably to someone behind her. The young woman blushed and dimpled with pleasure, while Lady Selina went scarlet with mortification.

'You are rather harsh, sir,' Margaret whispered when they were out of earshot.

'Not at all, ma'am. I always fit my manners exactly to my company.'

When supper was announced, Major Brummell escorted her to the Berrington table, and was promptly invited to remain himself. He divided his conversation between Margaret and his hostess, and it was only after supper, when the young Duke of Oxford had summoned up courage enough to ask Margaret for a second pair of dances, that Major Brummell at last quitted Margaret's side. She had no cause to question Mr Anderson's opinion of him.

Refusing to dance with the duke for the third time on the grounds of propriety, Margaret was escorted by him to Lady James, esconced again in the card-room. He showed no inclination to leave her then, and so they sat down on a sofa nearby, and talked quietly together.

Great was Margaret's astonishment when she saw Lord St George standing before her. He seemed to her completely as usual: polite, urbane, aloof.

'Miss Lambart, may I have the pleasure of leading you into the next dance?'

Margaret looked up at him, her own face a polite mask. But her thoughts were quite otherwise: turbulent and angry. How dare he ask her to dance after what she had overheard, and he must have known she had overheard! It was too much.

'Thank you, sir,' she said briefly, 'but I do not intend to dance any more tonight.'

She then turned back to the duke and resumed her conversation with him.

Margaret felt, but did not see the marquis stiffen, and in a moment turn away. The duke was looking at her with a very perturbed expression.

'You should h-have danced w-with St George, if you h-had liked it, M-Miss Lambart. *I* would not h-have minded, and h-he asks very few w-women to dance as a rule.'

'But I should *not* like it, I thank you, your Grace. I much prefer to stay here and talk with you — even in whispers, like this!'

'Do you really m-mean that, Miss Lambart?' the duke asked with boyish eagerness. 'Oh! You are the v-very best of f-fellows!'

6

The next morning Margaret was surprised by an early caller. When she heard the bell, she thought it must be the Duke of Oxford, come a little earlier than usual, but to her surprise, it was Major Brummell's name the maid announced.

Feeling distinctly pleased, Margaret tidied her hair, and hurried down to the drawing-room.

The major was attired all in grey, except for his dazzlingly white shirt and cravat. He was carrying a little posy of white rose-buds. He bowed when Margaret entered the room, and held the flowers out to her.

'When I saw them, Miss Lambart, I was reminded irresistably of yourself. I beg you to accept them from your most humble servant.'

'Oh, they are so pretty! Thank you very much, sir!'

Margaret took them with much pleasure.

'Pray, be seated, sir.'

Her visitor settled himself, and said, 'I am come to thank *you*, ma'am, for making yesterday evening such a delightful change. I — found myself in an exceedingly unusual situation, Miss Lambart.'

'Oh? And what was that, sir?'

'Normally, Miss Lambart, people seek my company for the good I can do them — for the influence I can exert in their favour. Oh, do not deny it, Miss Lambart. I am being neither modest — nor immodest; I state a fact. And I will let you into a secret, Miss Lambart, for I am certain that I can depend upon you. It amuses me very much, ma'am, to have those of so much higher birth and greater riches than I quailing at a mere look from me. But, yesterday I underwent a very unusual experience. I met someone who wanted nothing of me. Someone who, on her own admission, had neither position, nor riches, and yet who did not seek my help to be put in a position to attain either. In all the time I spoke with her, not once did she suggest I might do anything for her. I was much intrigued, I confess, Miss Lambart.'

'Oh, but sir — '

'I must say that, should she want these things, doubtless she would manage exceedingly well on her own; for it seems to me that she has already achieved a great deal before I was presented to her. She was natural and unaffected, and it was I who found myself wishing to impress *her*, rather than the usual reverse of the matter!'

'Oh, sir,' said Margaret, genuinely touched, but she could not go on. She did not know what she could say next, and she could merely look at her visitor with a shy smile.

Major Brummell himself said nothing for a few moments, but merely sat looking at her. Then he got up, crossed over to Margaret, and picking up one of her hands, he carried it to his lips.

'Now, Miss Lambart,' he said, briskly, straightening himself, 'I am come to ask you if I am to have the pleasure of seeing you at Almack's next week? It will be the first dance of the season.'

'As you know, Lady James does not go out much, sir. I doubt very much that we shall be there.'

'But would not you like to go? If you have a voucher for Almack's, Miss Lambart, you will have no further need of myself.'

'But, Major Brummell, I hope that we may always be friends!'

He bowed. 'And Almack's, ma'am? Would you like me to procure you a voucher for it? Lady Jersey is a great friend of mine.'

'So I have heard, sir.'

'Judging by the rest of your acknowledged acquaintance, from the egregious Mr Anderson, I presume?'

Margaret smiled. 'I cannot deny it, sir. And as for Almack's, I do not wish to put you out, sir.'

Major Brummell stared at her for a moment, then slowly shook his head. ''Faith, Miss Lambart — I sometimes — ' He stopped, and surveyed her again, then laughed. 'Most females, ma'am, would be jumping at the chance if I offered to procure them a voucher!'

Margaret hesitated. Then she spoke slowly, 'I will be frank with you, Major Brummell. As you no doubt realize, I am not used to high social life. In addition, I have not money enough to buy all the gowns and hats and shoes that I should need, were I to embark upon such a life. Even had I a voucher, sir, I do not know that I could use it.'

Major Brummell stared at her for a moment, then took a turn or two about the room.

'I had not thought, ma'am,' he said at last, 'that anyone had the power to astonish me so constantly.'

'I have not said anything very remarkable, sir! Only the truth!'

'The truth, I assure you, Miss Lambart, is the rarest of all commodities in London! You are a very remarkable woman, ma'am. Well, I shall send you a voucher, and leave you to decide whether or not you wish to use it. You will allow me to call upon you again?'

'Of course, sir; I am always happy to see my friends.'

Major Brummell bowed over her hand and departed. As the door was closing behind him, she heard a familiar voice say, 'Why, George!'

'Good day, St George,' she heard Major Brummell reply, and then the door closed. In another moment it opened again, and Joshua appeared to ask if she would see Lord St George.

'Is not his lordship desirous of seeing her ladyship?'

'He was asking for you, ma'am.'

Margaret had no wish to see the caller, but considered she should not refuse, as he was her godmother's nephew.

'Very well. Please show his lordship in.'

In a moment, Lord St George was before her. He bowed. Margaret curtseyed without smiling.

'I see that I am not your first visitor today, Miss Lambart.'

'Oh, no, sir. Major Brummell was here very early. Pray, sit down, Lord St George.'

Margaret seated herself, and waved her hand to a chair some distance from her own.

'My aunt, Lady James, is not over-tired, I trust?'

'Oh, no, sir; Lady James is in excellent spirits. You would wish to see her?'

'Not yet, I thank you, Miss Lambart.'

Lord St George paused, his eyes fixed on Margaret's face.

'I can see that last evening agreed with you also, Miss Lambart.'

'Yes, sir, I thank you. I enjoyed it — very much indeed.'

Margaret stared at him coolly.

Really, the man's effrontery was beyond anything! To say that the evening had agreed with her, after what she had overheard him say!

Lord St George looked round the room for some moments as if minutely examining every item of furniture and ornament there, as one who had not seen them before. Margaret felt a quiver of more than impatience.

'I think you asked to see me, my lord?'

He recollected himself, and looked at her. 'I beg your pardon, Miss Lambart; my mind — was wandering.'

Margaret inclined her head slightly, then looked at him questioningly, but still without a smile.

'You — er — find George Brummell pleasant company?' he asked.

'I believe he is generally considered to be very amusing, sir. I find him both excellent company and an extremely kind person.'

Lord St George's eyebrows moved a fraction upwards. 'Indeed? I had not known him noted for kindness.'

Margaret frowned a little, but said nothing. The marquis was silent for a moment, and then continued in a very matter-of-fact voice, 'You find the duke interesting company also, Miss Lambart?'

'The duke, sir?'

'My ward, Oxford.'

'Oh, yes, his grace is exceedingly interesting. I have learnt a great deal from him.'

The marquis's eyebrows rose again. 'You seem to take an unusual view of people, Miss Lambart. Although he is related to me by marriage, and I am his guardian still, I must admit that I had not found the duke a particularly interesting companion.'

Now Margaret's eyebrows rose, and she looked at the marquis as she might have looked at one of her younger sisters guilty of some social fault.

'That is hardly kind, sir! I cannot think you have ever, perhaps, taken the trouble to ask the duke his opinions upon subjects which interest him.'

Margaret was pleased to see that Lord St George looked amazed rather than anything else.

'Besides,' she went on, still in a tone of admonishment, 'his grace is still young, and suffers from perhaps the worst disadvantage that someone in society may suffer — shyness.' She looked at Lord St George a trifle maliciously. 'It does not seem to me that anyone has taken the trouble either to listen to, or to help his grace.'

His lordship looked as if he would say something, but instead paused, and when he did speak, it was in the same, matter-of-fact tone he had used before.

'You think shyness, I collect, the worst disadvantage in society, ma'am?'

'Oh, yes! If you think that lack of money or birth are greater disadvantages, I would reply that it seems to me that such a person would not ever be *in* society.'

'And yet it sometimes happens, ma'am!'

Margaret bowed her head in acquiescence.

'Indeed it does, sir. Major Brummell, I suppose one may say, is a case in point.'

'George Brummell is quite exceptional, ma'am. And yet, there are other examples.'

Margaret's eyes flashed, but she said equally enough, 'I am not sufficiently conversant with society, sir, to know to which examples you are now referring.'

Lord St George looked at her without replying. Then he said unexpectedly, 'I think you have been driving in the park with my ward, Oxford. He handles horses very well, does not he?'

'Again I cannot say, sir, as I do not know what constitutes handling horses well. He does not go so fast as to alarm me for our safety, nor so slow as to render the drive tedious. As far as I am concerned, the duke appears to be very skilful, and his driving suits me to perfection. For some others, doubtless, he would be too careful. Yet *they*, no doubt, consider themselves skilful with the reins. I have seen some phaetons — driven by both men and women, at what I can only describe as a reckless speed. Only the other day I saw one young woman knocked down by some creature who clearly thought that a very dashing figure was being cut, but who, in my view, was driving a great deal too fast for his capabilities. However dashing such a person may imagine himself, I can not find it in me to admire him one jot!'

'You are quite right, Miss Lambart,' Lord St George said, clearly a little dazed by her torrent of words, 'such a whip is reprehensible in the extreme.'

'I am glad you agree with me, sir. If persons of influence, such as yourself, would make known their disapproval, one might hope to make the park promenade rather pleasanter for everyone.'

There was another silence. Lord St George caught Margaret's eye from time to time, and Margaret returned his look, but made no attempt to break the silence.

'Your mother, Mrs Lambart,' the marquis said at last, 'and my aunt, Lady James, were school-fellows, I collect, ma'am?'

'That is so, sir.'

'But you have not seen Lady James very frequently, ma'am?'

'Unfortunately, no. But we have corresponded regularly ever since my mother's death. When I wrote to tell Lady James about the accident, she wrote back and said that she hoped we might keep up the connection, and, of course, I was happy to do so. In any case, Lady James *is* my godmother, and I should have considered it my duty to follow her wishes, whatever I may have felt. But, duty did not enter into it.'

'You set great store by duty, Miss Lambart?'

'Indeed, I do, sir!'

'My aunt, Lady James — is a very affectionate person, but she lives somewhat retired from the world, for all that she is in the middle of London, ma'am.'

'It seems to me, sir, that though Lady James may not venture out into society, she is well aware of most of what happens in it. I would not describe her as — an innocent, sir.'

'I should think not indeed, ma'am!' Lord St George said a little shortly. 'I see Lady James very frequently when I am in London, Miss Lambart, and have always done so!'

'So Lady James has told me, sir,' Margaret replied with a little smile. 'She has often told me how fond she is of you. She has, indeed, hopes of — '

Margaret stopped. No; she would not stoop to his depths. All his questions this morning, she could see, had been asked with one intention: that of finding out what she was about. Well, she would not compliment him by showing the same interest in his doings. She looked calmly at Lord St George. Now something seemed to have annoyed him. He wore an angry look, and his nostrils were quite pinched. Margaret felt pleased.

'Indeed!' Lord St George said in a constrained voice. 'I had not thought that Lady James would have discussed myself with you, Miss Lambart!'

'Oh, I should not dream of discussing you, sir,' Margaret said guilelessly, 'but Lady James naturally likes to talk about you, as you are her favourite nephew, and as I am here, it is quite natural that it is to me to whom she talks. But you need not feel offended, sir; she has told me nothing of any consequence about you. And were Lady James inadvertently to do so, I promise that nothing of it would ever be communicated to a third party.'

Lord St George did not look appeased. He rose from his seat.

'I came here today, ma'am, because I thought you were owed an apology. It was not my wish that you should overhear the conversation which took place between Lady Selina and myself — in fact, the whole episode was extremely unfortunate. But your conduct since my arrival, ma'am, has made me rethink my intention. Perhaps it is just as well that you should know that Lady James is not unprotected in the world!'

'It is as well, you mean, sir, that I should know that you suspect me of being an adventuress!' Margaret retorted coldly. 'I am very sorry, sir,' she went on sarcastically, 'that my conduct since your arrival should have given you cause to rethink your original gentlemanly intention. Your own conduct since your arrival, sir, had not led me to think that I should be likely to receive anything in the nature of an apology. Every question you have put to me, sir, has been tinged with impertinence!'

The marquis's face went white. 'I hardly think, ma'am, you have the right to accuse *me* of conduct unbecoming a gentleman. It would have been more ladylike, ma'am, if, yesterday evening, you had made your presence known!'

Margaret stared at him.

'I hardly think it behoves you, sir, to give lessons in correct behaviour. I did not 'make my presence known' last night, because I considered that there would be less embarrassment occasioned to all concerned if you and Lady Selina remained unaware that I was there. Had Major Brummell not returned when he did, both last night's discomfiture and today's — conversation — might have been avoided! But I have always been led to believe that it is the first duty of anyone in society — *good* society, that is — ' and Margaret's eyes flashed ominously here — 'to — keep the wheels oiled, so to speak, so that embarrassment is kept to the smallest possible minimum. *That*, sir, is why I did not make my presence known. And as for your impertinence, sir, in daring to think to instruct me in the usages of good society, I will tell you plainly, sir, that I have seen little of the conduct of a gentleman in your conduct towards me.'

Lord St George let out an exclamation at this, but Margaret gave him no time to speak. She swept on.

'It may be the conduct of a man of fashion, sir; *that* I am in no position to judge. But I assure you, sir, the veriest criminal would have been given more chance to exonerate themselves, than you were pleased to give me! When first we met, sir, you came here to look me over. Oh, yes, sir, I was perfectly well aware of what you were about! 'To look me over' expresses your attitude very precisely, I think.

'That might have been excusable, sir, in the circumstances, but not your attitude, sir, which was hostile from the first. And upon all our subsequent meetings, sir, including this present one, when your professed purpose in calling was to offer me an apology, your manner has been the same. You have quizzed me about my intentions, questioned my motives, and generally conducted all intercourse with me as though you were already convinced that I was a scheming hussy, intent upon alienating Lady James's affections from her own family — to induce her to settle as much of her money and her jewels upon me as possible — I think that would be your confederate, Lady Selina's claim; and for your own — to intrude myself into good society, depending upon Lady James's name and patronage for acceptance; and finally — that I have set my cap at his Grace of Oxford — I think, sir, that that is the phrase you would probably expect me to use! But before you took Lady Selina's story for truth, sir, you might, perhaps, have tried to get to know me a little — as did his Grace of Oxford. You might, perhaps, have asked him what he thought, for he is not the fool his family appear to think him!

'I would have you know, sir,' Margaret continued, taking breath, but allowing the marquis no time to get in a word, 'that, poor by your standards though I may be, I am a gentleman's daughter, and have never met such treatment in all my life! But for your peace of mind, my lord, though why it should concern me I am at a loss to understand, I will tell you that I have no designs upon your ward, nor upon Lady James's jewels, nor upon a great place in society! I have no wish at all to marry, and tell you so plainly. And that, sir, is the truth!'

Margaret ceased speaking, but continued to gaze coolly at the marquis, a slightly challenging expression in her eyes. The marquis for his part, stared back unmoving, not taking his eyes from her face. What he was thinking, Margaret could not divine: his face still wore its usual aloof look, and she could see no sign of any strong emotion. Margaret did not allow her eyes to waver, and at last the marquis spoke.

'Miss Lambart,' he said slowly, 'I — am near speechless . . .'

He paused. Margaret had throughout spoken quite calmly, though forcefully. She had not permitted her anger to control her. Now a slight frown creased her forehead.

'Indeed, sir?' she said coldly, as the marquis appeared to have no intention of continuing.

They might have continued staring at each other in silence for some time, had not a little clock at that moment chimed the half-hour. Margaret glanced across to it briefly, then turned back to the marquis.

'If you will excuse me, sir,' she said with formal politeness, 'I expect his grace about this time. Should you wish to speak to his grace, I will not descend immediately, in order to give you time to do so.'

Margaret curtseyed deeply, and with great dignity moved out of the room and closed the door gently behind her.

Only a few minutes later she heard Lord St George leave the house.

7

The following days saw a positive deluge of invitations being delivered at the house in Hanover Square. Lady James urged her to accept every one that came, but Margaret, knowing that the old lady found too many late evening parties very tiring, refused the greater part of them, and said that she much preferred spending her evenings with her godmother playing cards as she had done during her first weeks in London.

'I do not know most of these people, ma'am; I really cannot think why they should invite me.'

She said precisely the same to Major Brummell when he called upon her again.

'I did not see you at the Berwicks' reception last night, Miss Lambart.'

'No, sir; I was at cards with Lady Anderson.'

Major Brummell's eyebrows rose.

'Her ladyship was very disappointed, ma'am,' he said accusingly.

'But, sir,' Margaret exclaimed, 'I hardly know the countess!'

'You are unlikely to do so if you do not put yourself in the way of her company,' the Major said severely. 'I told the countess that her party could not be counted a first success as you had not consented to be present.'

'Oh, Major Brummell, you are too bad!' cried Margaret laughing. 'What possible difference could my presence or absence make?'

'It all depends upon what people *think*, dear Miss Lambart. If they *believe* your presence is essential to success, then it is.'

'Well, I think, then, sir, that you were very unkind to poor Lady Berwick. I am sure her party was quite delightful. And if what you say is true — for I am not deceived, sir, about the influence you wield — then I shall not dare refuse a single invitation, and that would be very distressing to poor Lady James.'

Major Brummell smiled.

'I know that you insist on thinking of yourself as among the dowagers, Miss Lambart, but your cleverness in marrying off your four sisters so creditably does not give you leave to do so. You are too great an ornament to society, ma'am, and I will not have you hiding yourself away. You are, frankly, Miss Lambart, like a breath of fresh country air.'

'Oh, I know exactly what you think of the country, sir,' said Margaret with a laugh. 'You can not wait to escape from it.'

'But the air, I like, ma'am. It is the *people* there who are such dumplings. Come, now, shall I see you at the Pulboroughs tonight?'

'I must say no, sir. I have promised to be at cards as usual.'

Major Brummell looked at her quizzically.

'Perhaps you are right, Miss Lambart,' he said slowly. 'Perhaps you are a great deal more — knowing — than I had thought you.'

'Whatever do you mean, sir?'

'That you are well aware of the value of aloofness, ma'am — you know that familiarity breeds contempt. If you appear but rarely, your presence will be valued all the more. Yes, that must be it. You are exceedingly clever, Miss Lambart. I congratulate you.'

'I assure you, sir, I thought no such thing!' Margaret cried hotly, greatly displeased and disappointed.

Major Brummell was on his knees beside her in a moment.

'I know! I know! Dear Miss Lambert! I was only joking! And in such very poor taste. Forgive me, I beg you.'

'I thought you knew me better than that, sir,' faltered Margaret.

'Oh, I do! Indeed I do! Say you forgive me quickly. I can not bear it when you look at me like that. I feel as if I had just — crushed a daisy under my heel.'

'Oh, get up, do, sir!' Margaret

laughed. 'My godmother, Lady James may come in, and to see you so might give her a very wrong impression.'

'Not till you say you have forgiven me, ma'am!'

'Oh, I forgive you! I forgive you! Only get up, do!'

Major Brummell seated himself on the sofa beside Margaret and pulled a small packet out of his pocket.

'This was the real purpose of my call, Miss Lambart. Here are two vouchers for Almacks — for yourself and for Lady James. I beg you to come on the first night. It is most important to be seen there then. Besides, I want you to meet my friend, Lady Jersey. She has heard a great deal about you, and is most anxious to meet you.'

'To look me over, you mean, sir?'

'You must know that that is the habit with newcomers, ma'am.'

'I was ungracious, forgive me, sir. As you wish it, I will certainly come.'

Major Brummell sat back and laughed out loud. Margaret looked at him enquiringly. Major Brummell wiped his eyes delicately.

'Oh, Miss Lambart! You are priceless! All over London there are young women who would give an arm for a voucher for Almack's, and you graciously condescend to be present as *I* wish it. Oh, Miss Lambart, you are magnificent!'

And he picked up both her hands and kissed them several times.

When Margaret opened the packet later, she found not only vouchers inside, but also the tickets necessary for entrance to the rooms.

★ ★ ★

Some two days before the Almack's opening evening, an imperious ring pealed through the house in Hanover Square. Margaret was sitting entertaining his Grace of Oxford in the small salon, and they could hear quite clearly what was going on. When the door was opened, Lady Selina's angry voice was heard demanding, 'Where is Miss Lambart, Joshua? I must speak with her immediately!'

'Miss Lambart is in the small salon, my lady,' came Joshua's measured tones. 'Miss Lambart is at present engaged, my lady. I will go upstairs and enquire — '

'There is no need for that, Joshua!' cried Lady Selina; 'I can find my way myself.'

'But, my lady — !'

There was the sound of hasty footsteps ascending the staircase. In another moment the door of the small salon burst open and Lady Selina stood in the doorway, her face a mask of anger. Margaret had risen to greet her, and Lady Selina stared at her, not at first noticing the duke behind her.

'How dare you!' she shouted. 'How dare you! You nobody, you! You come here, trying to sneak your way into the affections of my aunt, you who are nothing to her! A mere nobody from the country! A female Johnny

Raw! You worm your way in here, crawling to be received into decent society, kissing my aunt's hand — 'yes, your ladyship', 'no your ladyship', 'may I borrow your jewels, your ladyship' — 'oh, yes, your ladyship, only the best ones, your ladyship, — the pearls, your ladyship — ' '

At this moment Lady Selina caught sight of her brother.

'And now you have the impertinence to cast a spell over my brother, his Grace of Oxford, so that he cannot do a thing but you must approve it! 'Miss Lambart likes a blue coat very well', 'Miss Lambart likes plain gold buttons', 'Miss Lambart has seen the new Lincolnshire sheep in Cheshire and thinks they would do very well for me!' Oh, yes, you have insinuated your way into his confidence very cleverly, poor fool that he is! You, who are old enough to be his mother! And now, to cap all, from sheer spite — or perhaps to show your new power — you have had my voucher at Almack's cancelled!

You have got George Brummell to cancel my voucher. Oh, how dare you! If my brother had an ounce of manhood in him,' she went on with a glare at the duke, 'he would support me now, would take *my* part, but, of course he does not — you — you — ladybird, you!'

Margaret was so completely astonished by this attack that for a moment her wits quite left her, and she merely stood where she was. Her mind slowly grasped hold of the last accusation.

'Indeed, Lady Selina,' she gasped, 'you are quite mistaken. I have done no such thing.'

'Of course you must have done! Why else should my voucher be cancelled? Because of what happened at the Berringtons' I suppose. Well, you deserved to hear! You deserved to know what people in good society are saying about you — an adventuress come to ingratiate yourself among them — you are a nobody: no birth, no blood, no breeding, no money. You have no right to be here. And when you do appear, it is in borrowed jewels — to which you have no right. How dare you do this to me! You upstart! You — you — Cyprian, you!'

The duke stood up, his face now red with anger.

'Silence!' he said in a terrible voice.

His sister took no notice.

'I will see that you will not be received in any house in London!' Lady Selina stormed. 'I will tell them all what you are. Doors everywhere will be closed in your face, and you will be left to sit in the gutter — which is your natural home. I will — '

'I said 'Silence!' Selina,' the duke said in the same terrible voice. 'If you do not at once obey me, you shall go back to Darrington where you will stay, and you will never again be permitted to cross the threshold of my house in Berkeley Street.'

It can only be said now that Lady Selina's eyes bulged.

'But — but — ' she stammered.

She stared at her brother.

'Now, apologise to Miss Lambart,' the duke continued in the same manner.

Lady Selina stood there with her mouth opening and shutting, staring from her brother to Margaret and back again.

'Never!' she gasped, in a stifled voice.

'I said apologise!' thundered the duke.

His sister remained silent. He took a step towards her.

'I — I beg your pardon, Miss Lambart,' gasped Lady Selina, still staring at her brother.

'I know there is no truth in any of the accusations I have made,' went on the duke.

There was silence.

'Say it!' he thundered again.

'I — know that there is no — no truth at all — in — '

' — in any of the accusations I have made,' prompted the duke.

His sister repeated the words in a daze.

'I humbly beg your pardon — '

There was silence again.

'Say it!'

'I humbly beg your pardon.'

'I know that I have grievously injured you, and will endeavour to put right any harm I may have done you.'

Lady Selina repeated this very quickly.

'And now you may go,' ordered the duke, waving his hand in a lordly way.

His sister stared at him in silence for a moment, then slowly curtseyed to Margaret and then to her brother. After that, she turned and rushed from the room, and Margaret clearly heard a sob escape her as she ran down the stairs.

The duke remained standing and continued to stare at the door. Then very slowly he sat down, his face coloured, and he looked as astonished as his sister had done before. He looked towards Margaret.

'I — I beg your pardon, Miss Lambart; I should never have spoken in that manner in front of you. It was grossly improper.'

He stood up.

'I do not know to what my sister referred — what happened at the Berringtons' — but I collect that you were, in some way, insulted by my sister.' The duke paused, and seemed to be making an effort to speak normally. 'I hope, ma'am, that you will permit me to call upon you again — to apologise — when I — when I am more in command of myself.'

'Of course, sir,' Margaret said, also making an effort to sound as usual. 'You know that I will be very glad to welcome you at any time.' And she gave the duke a warm smile.

The duke looked at her, his face troubled.

'Miss Lambart,' he said in a choked voice, 'you are the kindest, noblest, dearest creature in the world, and — I would not have had this happen for anything! Pray excuse me, ma'am.'

He took Margaret's hand and held it for several moments while he gazed deeply into her eyes; then he lifted her hand to his lips. He gave her another long look, then turned and walked steadily to the door and went out.

★ ★ ★

When Margaret next saw Major Brummell, which was later that very same day, immediately she brought up the matter of Lady Selina's cancelled voucher.

'I cannot think that you are responsible, sir,'

Major Brummell stretched out one hand and inspected his beautifully polished nails.

'I am not quite certain that I understand you, ma'am.'

'You are aware that Lady Selina Cumnor's voucher for Almack's has been cancelled, sir?'

'It has been mentioned to me,

certainly, Miss Lambart.'

'I hope it is not widely known,' said Margaret quickly.

'Surely that should not upset you, ma'am?'

'Anything which touches the honour of his Grace of Oxford to his detriment upsets me, sir. I would not wish his grace to suffer any distress. It would, therefore, please me very much, sir, if you would use your influence with the patronesses of Almack's — with Lady Jersey — to get Lady Selina's voucher restored.'

'I really do not see why you should ask me to do that, ma'am. In any case, I doubt I have the influence.'

'Oh, come, sir! I know what a friend you are to Lady Jersey. I have, indeed, heard how indebted to you the lady is — for standing by her. She would do anything for you, I am told.'

Margaret looked enquiringly at him, but Major Brummell made no answer, merely regarding her from under his half-closed eyelids.

'Please, sir,' Margaret pleaded, 'it would be a great relief to me if you would endeavour to get Lady Selina's voucher restored. As a favour to me, sir?'

'She does not at all deserve it, Miss Lambart.'

'But you will try, sir?' persisted Margaret.

'Very well; as you ask me so particularly, I will do what I can.'

Margaret was about to thank him very warmly, but he held up his hand to stop her before she spoke.

'But *not* for the first ball of the season. *That* I will not do, Miss Lambart; I am determined, quite determined that Lady Selina shall suffer something.'

'But — then everyone will know that it has been cancelled, and that is what I wish to avoid!' Margaret cried.

'She may say that she is unwell and unable to attend.'

'Please!' Margaret begged.

'No, Miss Lambart, Lady Selina

must be taught a lesson. Besides, from what I have heard, she is not fit to come.'

Margaret, remembering the scene earlier in the day, could not find it in her heart to protest at this. However, she did urge him again to relent, but Major Brummell remained adamant, and Lady Selina did indeed have to resort to the subterfuge of claiming to have the headache on the evening of the first Almack ball, and she did not appear in the rooms until the second ball of the season.

As for Margaret herself, when the evening arrived, she viewed her appearance at Almack's with a great deal of misgiving. Indeed, had she not told Major Brummell quite positively that she would be there, she might well have decided to spend the evening at the card table. The reason for this disinclination was that she knew she must see Lord St George there. But when she was dressed, and once again adorned in Lady James's pearls, which she had only agreed to because of her ladyship's pleas, she began to hope that the evening might pass off reasonably well.

Major Brummell was waiting to greet herself and Lady James when they arrived, and at once presented them to the five patronnesses. Margaret was not at all sure what she had expected, but certainly not this set of plain, and on the whole elderly women, who would not have won a second glance in Cheshire!

Turning from the five after receiving some gracious words from them, Margaret was a little perturbed to see Lord St George approaching. But he greeted her as if nothing untoward had ever passed between them, and showed not the slightest inclination to leave them when his duty to his aunt was done. Indeed, when the orchestra struck up, she was somewhat put out to hear him asking her for the first dance. The idea of near an hour's tête-à-tête with him was not something she could contemplate with any pleasure, but with Major Brummell still deep in conversation with Lady James, short of an open slight, Margaret had no course but to accept his offer. She could not think why he was choosing to behave in this quite unexpected way! None of her rehearsed schemes for her conduct when encountering him again had prepared her for this. Resignedly she laid her hand upon his proferred arm as lightly as she could and, with ramrod back walked beside him to the set, her thoughts in some confusion.

While they were waiting for all the dancers to find places, Margaret determined not to be the first of them to speak. She was conscious that the marquis was watching her very intently, but she pretended to be unaware of this, and looked at the sets being formed with forced interest. But at last, she found herself quite unable to avoid looking at him directly.

As soon as he caught her eye, the marquis said very gravely, 'This time,

Miss Lambart, I wish to offer my apology immediately, before — ' He paused for a moment, and a slight smile touched his lips, 'before anything untoward happens,' he finished. 'I wish to say that I know how ill I have behaved towards you, quite mistakenly, as I now believe, and I regret it very much. I hope you will forgive me?'

Margaret was too surprised to respond at once.

'Miss Lambart?' the marquis said after a moment.

'I beg your pardon, sir,' Margaret replied, looking directly at him, 'I was deliberating how I should reply. For the sake of my godmother, I accept your apology — which I may say I think I deserve, and for her sake, I will endeavour to put the past quite behind me. More than that, I can not promise — ' She paused, and added after a moment, 'I think it best to be quite honest, sir.'

The marquis inclined his head gravely at this.

'I must tell you that I cannot be completely easy with you, sir, and I think it would be best if we maintained the manners of the slightest of acquaintances,' Margaret finished firmly.

She thought she saw the corners of the marquis's mouth twitch, but she could not be sure. She looked up into his eyes sharply, but he seemed quite grave.

'I think you have hit on an admirable solution, ma'am. I am grateful for your indulgence, and accept your conditions most gratefully.'

They danced together for the requisite two dances very sedately, and then Lord St George led her back to Lady James who was now deep in conversation with an old friend she had just rediscovered. Margaret had expected the marquis to excuse himself once she was safely by her godmother's side, but he did not, and, positioning himself behind his aunt's chair, he rested one hand on its gilt back, and with the other held his glass. From time to time, he bent down towards Margaret and made some remark, all of them the veriest commonplaces.

'The music is quite delightful, is not it, Miss Lambart?'

'Indeed it is, sir,' Margaret agreed.

'It is becoming quite a crush here now, is not it, Miss Lambart?'

'Indeed it is, sir.'

'I shall look forward to the tea, shall not you, Miss Lambart?'

'Indeed, I shall, sir.'

His presence made Margaret distinctly uncomfortable, and she wished very much that he would go away and talk to somebody else, but, far from this, he appeared to be quite rooted to the spot.

When the next dance began, a gentleman appeared before them — one of those whom Major Brummell had presented to her at the Duchess of Berrington's ball — and begged Lady James's permission to lead Miss Lambart out. With a great deal of relief

Margaret accepted his arm. Throughout the dance, she kept her eye upon Lord St George, hoping — expecting to see him move from his station, but he did not. He appeared as immovable as ever, and when her partner at last returned her to her place, he bowed to her partner in what Margaret thought crossly was a grossly proprietorial way.

Margaret was asked out again, and when she returned, the marquis had still not moved. He greeted her with a polite smile, made one or two more commonplace remarks, and subjected the next gentleman who approached to request the honour of Miss Lambart's hand in the dance to a severe quizzing.

When the supper was announced, he offered his arm to Lady James, and Margaret saw that she was not to be rid of him yet. With misgivings, she suspected that he would remain beside her for the whole of the evening. Why could not he dance with someone else?

She was rather more pleased when

Major Brummell appeared at her side, and greeted him with a wide smile. The four of them then moved into the supper-room, and Margaret thought she saw a glint of amusement in Major Brummell's eye as he asked, 'Well, ma'am, and how have you been enjoying your first visit to Almack's?'

'To tell you the truth, sir,' Margaret replied in a voice loud enough for the marquis to hear quite plainly, 'I have found it a little — commonplace! I have had more interesting evenings in a secluded Cheshire manor-house.'

Major Brummell looked down at her in mock surprise.

'You astonish me, Miss Lambart! The cream of London society! The very pick of fashion! The absolutely hautest of the ton! What can you mean?'

'I mean sir, that if this is the best London society can provide, I have found better conversations at home!'

'Indeed! I had always thought Lord Perowne an amusing and cultivated fellow!'

'He is a great rattle, and he is certainly amusing, sir,' admitted Margaret. 'I regret there are not more like him.'

'Was he the *only* agreeable interlude, then, Miss Lambart?'

Margaret looked at Major Brummell severely, then broke into a laugh. 'I know perfectly well, sir, that you are trying to — roast me. But it would not be becoming in me to tell you what I think, so I will only remind you that I have been unaccustomed to chaperonage — of any kind — for longer than I care to remember. I find the sensation — very strange!'

She was still smiling as she said this, but she looked at him warningly. She had, suddenly, a strong suspicion that Major Brummell was enjoying a joke which she did not understand fully, but which she could make a guess at. She stared at the marquis's back with a determined eye, and when they came to the supper table, adroitly managed to seat herself away from him, and had the satisfaction of seeing that he looked somewhat put out.

After supper, the marquis took up his position as before, and Margaret danced first in the second half with Major Brummell. The marquis himself requested the next dance, and Margaret graciously accepted, still on her guard, and quite smilingly polite. When once or twice, she thought the conversation was tending towards something other than commonplaces, she firmy brought it back. She was beginning to enjoy the game.

The evening ended with Margaret having danced every dance, all of them with Corinthians of the first water, and she could not but be aware that she had attracted attention, particularly from some of the mammas of daughters not so happily employed. She realized suddenly that, in retrospect, she had enjoyed the evening a very great deal, and decided that Almack's was not such a bad place after all. She said as much to Major Brummell.

He did not even attempt to keep his face straight.

'As I have said many times before, Miss Lambart, you are magnificent! What say you, St George?'

The marquis inclined his head in agreement.

'Miss Lambart is, indeed, remarkable!'

8

The morning after her appearance at Almack's, a huge basket of syringa bossom arrived for Margaret in Hanover Square. Its heavy scent filled the hall, but there was no note to be found to say who might have sent such a lavish gift. Margaret smiled to herself. It must be from his Grace of Oxford, it seemed the sort of extravagant gesture the young man might make, and she knew he had been down to his estate in Kent with his sister for the last days. Lord St George had offered this piece of intelligence last night during their second pair of dances; the flowers must mean that he was returned.

As if in answer to her thoughts, the duke arrived very shortly afterwards.

'Oh, your Grace!' Margaret exclaimed when he was shown into the room. 'How glad I am to see you again!'

She held out her hand to him. 'The flowers are so beautiful; I do thank you for them. Their scent makes the house like a summer garden.'

'I — I am afraid I did not send them, Miss Lambart,' the duke replied with something like a blush. 'I deeply regret it.'

'Then I wonder who can have done so? Oh, it was probably Major Brummell. But how glad I am to see you again; pray do sit down.'

'Thank you, ma'am,' the duke said with obvious difficulty, 'but, with your permission, I prefer to stand.'

'Oh?' Margaret smiled up at him. 'As you like. I — I trust you found all well in Kent?'

'Yes, I thank you, ma'am; all — was in excellent order.'

The duke's stammer had not reappeared, but he was very hesitant, and the colour came and went in his face. Margaret wondered how she might put him at ease.

'I hope you were able to take your

ride, sir, before the rain began.'

'I — we — have but just returned, ma'am.'

The duke began to stride about the room. Margaret wondered what it could possibly be that he found so difficult to say. Whatever his hesitancies had been before, she had never seen him quite like this.

'Pray, sir, do tell me what it is — '

'Miss Lambart, I have something to — ' the duke began at exactly the same moment.

They stopped together. Margaret smiled.

'Pray, proceed, sir.'

'No, no, Miss Lambart. I beg you — '

'I had nothing of any consequence to say, sir. I was only about to remark that you have not found it so difficult to talk to me before.'

The duke stared at her, the colour coming and going in his face. Then he took a deep breath.

'I-I must apologise, ma'am, fort — leaving London so abruptly, and for sending you no message. I-I know that it is not the custom — but — but — in the circumstances — ' His voice trailed away.

'Oh, your Grace, pray do not give it another thought. You needed — time for reflection, sir; I understood that.'

Margaret risked the reference to the events of a few days ago; the duke must wish to refer to them, so obviously ill-at-ease was he, and yet he seemed quite unable to broach the subject himself.

He stood staring at her in silence, the colour still coming and going in his countenance. Then he took a deep breath, strode up to Margaret, and stopped a few inches from her.

'Miss Lambart, you know that I think you the most wonderful woman in the world: the kindest, the most forgiving, the most beautiful — '

Margaret tried to protest, but the duke raced on.

'Yes, beautiful,' he said firmly. 'You have such grace, Miss Lambart, in everything you do. No — one else would have been so magnanimous as you: such insults as you received, and your graciousness to me! No words can ever adequately express what I feel, dear Miss Lambart! I shall ever be in your debt.'

'Indeed, sir, there is no need to feel any such thing. It is all in the past now,' said Margaret kindly. 'You must put it aside; forget it.'

'Never! I can never forget it! Nor do I wish to!'

Suddenly the duke knelt down beside her and took hold of both her hands.

'I wish always to remember your greatness of mind — to have it before me always. I wish always to protect you — I promise more adequately than on the last occasion! In short, Miss Lambart, I wish for nothing else but to spend my life worshipping you. I have loved you, I think, since the first moment I saw you, and — I have the great honour, Miss Lambart, to ask you to be my wife!'

Margaret was so surprised by this

unexpected declaration that for a moment she knew not what to say. She had known, of course, that the duke was fond of her, but never for one moment had she suspected — ! How very blind, she must have been! And yet, Lady Selina —

The duke, who had been staring at her face very intently, his lips trembling, suddenly bent his head and pressed kisses on her hands.

'Stop, sir! I beg you!' Margaret cried, gently trying to withdraw her hands.

But the duke clutched them still and pressed them against his heart.

'Margaret, dearest Margaret, say that you will indeed be my wife!'

Margaret looked at the eager, expectant eyes and the feverish brow.

'Oh, my dear,' she said in a low voice, 'my very dear duke.'

She tried to smile at him, but it was a tremulous effort. She did, however, manage to free one of her hands, and put it to the duke's forehead and smoothed back the hair. The young man's forehead was indeed burning. 'Surely,' she said with a little rallying smile, 'you cannot think I would make a very suitable duchess!'

'You are the only woman I want for my duchess!' he cried impetuously. 'There is no woman I have ever met who can compare with you. Noble, beautiful, what more can any man want?'

Margaret shook her head.

'It cannot be,' she said softly.

The duke looked stricken.

'Margaret!'

She shook her head again.

'Come and sit beside me, and I will tell you why.'

He stared at her with burning eyes, then, without moving his glance, he did as she bade him, still holding her one hand. She covered his hands with her free one.

'My dear,' she said, 'never shall I receive a greater honour than you have just paid me. I shall always be sensible of the compliment — not only because of your great title, but because I value your friendship. You, too, are kind, and generous — and intelligent,' Margaret added with a little smile. 'You — have not thought the worst of me, though doubtless you, too, might have been expected to think the same. I hold you in the highest esteem — the very highest esteem. You are, my dear, exactly the sort of man I would choose to marry, had I the choice. But — I have no choice, in this.'

'But you have! You have! I offer myself to you!' the duke cried almost wildly; 'Choose me!'

Margaret could feel the hands she held in hers trembling. She shook her head again.

'I am very attached to you, sir. Your honour and your welfare are very precious to me. But, my affection for you — ' The duke's look of eagerness as she said this quickly faded as she continued, ' — is not the affection a wife should bear her husband: the love you deserve from your wife! I do not have that love to give you, sir, however much I might wish that it could be. My love for you is — is the love of a sister; not that of a woman to stand by your side throughout her life.'

The duke stared at her for a moment, then turned away from her.

'You love another!' he said miserably.

'No, indeed not! I love no one! There is no one else.'

Margaret thought she heard the duke say 'Mr Brummell' under his breath. She could not help smiling in amusement.

'Oh, my dear duke, Major Brummell is my friend! He can never be anything more. Nor do I wish it.'

The duke turned back to her eagerly, struck by a hopeful thought.

'Perhaps you could come to love me?'

'Oh, do not hope for that, I beg you.'

'But in time — '

'Time!' repeated Margaret. 'Ah, there, perhaps you have it!'

'How do you mean?'

Margaret looked at him, smiling.

'How old are you, sir?'

'Twenty,' he answered quickly; then more slowly, 'nearly twenty.'

'So, not yet twenty. And still the ward of Lord St George, I think. And have you any idea how old I am?'

'Twenty-three?' the duke said tentatively. 'No, no! Twenty-two; perhaps twenty-one!'

Margaret laughed aloud.

'You flatter me exceedingly! Twenty-two, perhaps twenty-one! I cannot think what Lady Selina could say were she to hear that! My dear — I am — twenty-*seven*!'

'But that is not so old!'

Margaret laid her hand against the duke's cheek.

'Dear David — do you realize that I was out when you were scarcely out of your short coats?' She smiled again. 'Beside you, I am a hundred years old!'

'You called me David! Say it again!

Call me David again!'

'David.'

'Dear David!'

'Dear David,' she repeated.

He gripped her hands again.

'There will never be anyone else!'

'Indeed, I trust you may be wrong! I do not wish to see you spend your life alone.'

The duke shook his head. 'Never. I shall never meet another with your nobility of mind.'

'Nobility of mind can become very tiring!' Margaret said in a teasing voice. 'It is not at all necessary for a marriage, I assure you. No; you must look about you for a pleasant young woman, pretty and with some intelligence — for I would not have you saddled with a fool — but who will look up to you and think you the most wonderful man in the world.'

The duke sighed and looked melancholy.

'Do one thing for me then, I beg you,' he said in a low voice.

'What is it?'

'Call me always David — as a sign of our friendship.'

Margaret shook her head. 'It would not be at all proper, sir. What would your wife think?'

'I have no wife. Please — I like to hear it on your lips.'

Margaret considered a moment. 'Perhaps, sometimes, I may do so — when we are alone. But only then. If people heard me so addressing you in public, the suspicions I have already engendered would be magnified a thousandfold!'

'I — I had not thought of that,' the duke answered in a low voice. He stood up and heaved a great sigh. 'You — you will drive with me in the park again, will not you, Miss Lambart? You will not — because — '

'If you wish it. But for your own sake, I think it would be better if we stopped the habit.'

'Please!' he begged.

'Dear David.' Margaret stood on

tiptoe and kissed his cheek. 'Now, when you leave me, you are not to be wretched. You are to tell yourself that you do not care a fig for that creature, and think how exceedingly awkward it would have been if you had been taken at your word! Then you must look about for the prettiest creature you can find, and take *her* for a drive in your curricle, and make every head turn with admiration and not astonishment!'

'Do not speak so!' The duke looked stricken. 'I can never look at anyone else!'

'But you must! You must! You must come to love someone nearer your own age. I am far too old for you! You must think of me as an older sister.'

'I wish I *had* such a sister,' the duke said morosely.

★ ★ ★

Margaret was so discomposed by the duke's proposal, for which she blamed herself very much, that she gave orders to say that she had the headache and would see no other callers. She thus turned away St George. But after a short drive, the fresh air restored her to her usual equanimity, and on her return, being greeted by the news that Lady Grampian was waiting to see Lady James, she recognized at once the name of Lord St George's sister, and hurried upstairs to meet her with a good deal of curiosity. She found a slight girl in a muslin gown and a gypsy bonnet staring out of the window, who turned as Margaret came in. The girl's eyes grew wide.

'Oh! You must be — ' the girl gasped.

'I am Margaret Lambart,' Margaret said composedly, curtseying. 'I am sorry there was no one to receive you when you arrived, Lady Grampian. But I daresay Lady James will not be long now.'

'How do you do?' the girl said, looking at Margaret with interest as she returned the curtsey. 'I have been waiting already near a full half hour; I dare say my aunt is making me wait on purpose.'

'Why should she do that, ma'am?' Margaret said, quite astonished. 'Oh, I beg your pardon,' she went on hurriedly, 'but Lady James is not accustomed to rise early.'

The girl leaned towards Margaret with a conspiratorial smile.

'I know that. But I am sure my aunt is keeping me waiting because she does not approve of me.'

'Not approve of you, Lady Grampian!'

The girl shook her head, still smiling.

'Oh, indeed, ma'am, I am sure you are quite mistaken!' Margaret exclaimed. 'I have heard Lady James say a dozen times how very happy she is now that you are married.'

'Oh, they are all glad that I am married! They all wished me to settle down! They have each of them told me, on a great many occasions, how exceedingly lucky I am that Grampian so dotes upon me.'

'I should not have thought that would be difficult,' said Margaret, frankly eyeing the pretty creature before her.

The girl gave a gurgling little laugh and returned Margaret's look.

'And so you are the — unknown Miss Lambart,' she said after a moment. 'I must say that you do not look very terrifying to *me*.'

'Terrifying!'

'Yes. Selina gave me to understand that you were quite a dragon and that you — '

Lady Grampian stopped suddenly, blushed, and put one hand to her mouth.

'Oh, I do beg your pardon, Miss Lambart! I should never have said that, but it quite slipped out! I had expected something so very different, you see, and, as I say, you do not look at all the — '

Lady Grampian stopped again abruptly.

'The — er — adventuress you had

expected?' Margaret said with a teasing smile, but a rather grim look in her eye.

Lady Grampian blushed.

'Oh, no, dear Miss Lambart! Nothing so bad as that! But — but — ' she went on, anxious to make amends, ' — I had expected someone a great deal older, and with a vast quantity of rouge, and with — with — '

Margaret rubbed her cheeks with the tips of her fingers, and then spread out her hand before Lady Grampian.

'You will see, ma'am, as the Lady Olivia says, ' 'Twill endure wind and weather!' '

Lady Grampian stared at Margaret for a moment, and then burst out laughing.

'Oh, Miss Lambart, I do like you! I like you exceedingly!'

'But you know nothing about me!'

'Indeed I do! I know that you have four sisters, all younger than you, and now all married. I know that you come from — from Cheshire, and that this is the first time that you have been in London, and that somehow you have acquired great influence with Mr Brummell, and that Selina does not care for that at all — in fact, you would not believe how put out she is. And I know that you have been very often driving with David Oxford — Selina does not like that either, and that you are a very good hand at whist, and — ' The girl paused for breath.

'That is indeed a lot,' said Margaret, amused, 'and you certainly have the advantage of me. I am afraid that I know nothing at all of you, beyond the fact that you are recently married.'

'Well, there you have it,' the other girl said simply; 'there is no more to know. Grampian has carried me off to his Highland eyrie and we have but just returned to London now. Do you know, Miss Lambart, it has taken us near four weeks to make the journey? Grampian would travel in his coach with all our luggage coming in waggons behind us. We made quite a procession I assure you. I wanted him to let us come forward in his curricle, but he would not hear of it. He said he wished to make the journey as his father had always done, but oh, it was so slow! I was near dead with fatigue and boredom. Still, we are here now, for at least eight weeks, and after that, I hope St George will ask us to go to Whitebrook; it is so beautiful in the autumn. The trees are all so full in Oxfordshire. In Scotland there are scarce any trees at all.'

'I have never ventured into Scotland, Lady Grampian.'

'Then do not do it, Miss Lambart. I advise you most strongly not to do it. It is a wild, savage place still. Oh, it is very beautiful, I am sure, and I dare say Mr Gilpin would think very well of it, but it is quite a different matter to live there always.' The girl sighed, then said in more robust tones, 'There! Now you know all about me, and as you see, it is not so very much. But tell me, did you really wear the Hellington pearls to a ball?'

'Lady James was so kind as to lend me some jewels as I have none of my own.'

'None?' the girl sounded astonished.

Margaret shook her head with a little smile.

'No jewels at all?'

'No.'

'Then how have you managed?'

Margaret could not help laughing.

'Where I live, Lady Grampian, we do not have many balls.'

'But — your mother — !'

'I had to sell my mother's jewels long ago — to provide dowries for my sisters.'

'*You* had to provide dowries for your sisters!'

'Who else should have done so, ma'am?'

'But — your uncles! Your other kinsfolk?'

'We are quite horridly short of such advantages, Lady Grampian.'

'*I* should be glad for it! You cannot think what it is like to have Selina Cumnor always trying to bully you! That is partly why I married Grampian; so that I should have precedence of her!'

'Now, I do not believe for one moment that that is true!'

'No. You are quite right! It is not true. I am indeed exceedingly attached to Grampian. But I am still particularly glad that he is a marquis, like St George, and not a mere earl. Selina wants to marry St George, you know. I hope to goodness he will not have her!'

★ ★ ★

The marquis himself appeared again in Hanover Square, shortly after his sister had departed. Now, Margaret felt quite able to receive him, and indeed, after the first greetings had been done, and they had spoken a little about Lady Grampian, Margaret saying amiably how very delightful she had thought her, it was plain to Margaret that of the two of them, it was his lordship who was a great deal the more discomposed.

He paced the room, clearly wishing to say something, and equally clearly not knowing how to do it. Margaret watched him, wondering what could be on his mind.

'Miss Lambart, forgive me if I speak plainly,' he at last blurted out. 'Earlier today I met with young Oxford, my ward. He — he has told me everything, Miss Lambart. Your — your good sense, your — dignity — are beyond praise!'

Margaret said with dignity, 'You are very kind, sir!'

'Ah, Miss Lambart,' the marquis continued, 'do not be bitter, I pray! I told you before I had this latest intelligence that I knew I had been completely mistaken in my view of you! I wrote it in my note!'

'Your note, sir! What note? I have

received no note.'

'I ventured to send one with the flowers, Miss Lambart. In view of what I wished to say, I hoped you would forgive the impropriety. I also expressed the hope that you would receive me today so that I might explain personally —'

'And when you came I sent a message that I had the headache! Oh, sir, I beg you will forgive me! But I did not know from whom the flowers came — I thought perhaps Major Brummell had sent them. But I received no note with them!'

The marquis stared at her, clearly much disturbed.

'It must have been lost!' he exclaimed. 'Unless — no! I could not forget to attach it!'

Lord St George looked so upset as he said this, that Margaret felt quite sorry for him. She said with a slight teasing smile, 'I fear you must have spent a great deal of time composing it, sir, if its non-delivery so perturbs you!'

'I had thought my path was half-made when I came here, and now — Oh, Miss Lambart!'

He looked so rueful as he spoke that Margaret could not help smiling. The marquis looked at her despairingly for a moment, then suddenly smiled, too, and in a moment they both laughed.

'Miss Lambart,' the marquis said after a moment, still smiling but yet earnest, 'may we start again?'

'Again? How do you mean, sir?'

'As if we had just met, Miss Lambart.'

'Would that be quite wise, sir?'

The marquis laughed again. 'I meant as if we had never met and had heard nothing of each other.'

Margaret felt unaccountably pleased. She held out her hand.

'With all my heart, sir.'

The marquis caught hold of her hand gladly.

'And to seal our pact, ma'am, will you drive out in the park with me today?'

Margaret hesitated.

'But — you have refused my ward, ma'am. Is there any reason why *I* should not drive you now?'

'N-no, sir.' The girl hesitated a moment. 'Thank you. I shall be very glad to come with you. And I must thank you also for the flowers. I — have never received so many in my life before!'

The marquis bowed. The expression on his face seemed to say that he would have been mightly put out had it been otherwise.

And when later that day Margaret found herself seated beside Lord St George in the phaeton he still liked to drive, she felt a great deal more agitated than she ever remembered feeling when driving with the duke. She had dressed with particular care, and in honour of the occasion she had put on a new pink carriage dress and a bonnet with a long, curling ostrich feather which swept round to frame her face.

The marquis had at once complimented Margaret upon her bonnet and this had made her feel unusually shy, but once seated in the carriage and driving through the bustling streets which never bored her, Margaret was soon in command of herself again.

Their first circuit of the promenade was unremarkable. The phaeton was, of course, higher than the Duke of Oxford's curricle to which Margaret was accustomed, and she found the higher view delightful. She was conscious that to every horseman and carriage that passed them they were an object of curiosity if not astonishment, and Lord St George was forever raising his hat. Indeed, it seemed to be more off his head than on, and there was little opportunity for consecutive conversation.

At one point Margaret caught sight of Major Brummell with a rather portly gentleman, both of them mounted. She was very conscious of the major's astonished stare before he raised his hat and smiled and bowed in his usual elegant fashion. The portly gentleman beside him did the same. As for the marquis, he not only raised his hat, but bowed quite from the waist. Margaret herself bowed to the major and glanced at his companion, and then they were past them.

'Well, and what did you think of him then?' the marquis asked with a smile.

'Of whom? Oh, you mean the person with Major Brummell? I did not notice him very much, sir, but, I must say, if he wishes to be fashionable, I am afraid he will have to lose one or two of his chins.'

The marquis swallowed a laugh.

'I am not at all sure, ma'am, that that is not Lèse-Majesté!'

Margaret stared at him uncomprehendingly for a moment, then an appalled expression spread over her face.

'Do you mean, sir, that — that — ?'

The marquis nodded, his eyes gleaming.

'Oh! Why did not you tell me, sir? I have not seen him before and — Oh! What can he have thought! I barely bowed. Oh, I shall never hold my head up again.'

'This is most unlike you, ma'am!'

'How do you mean, sir?'

'To be overset by such a little matter,' the marquis said, eyeing Margaret's flushed cheeks with interest. 'I must say, ma'am,' he went on, 'it is quite amazingly becoming.'

'You can hardly call it a little matter practically to cut the Prince!'

The marquis was about to reply when he swerved quickly to avoid a smart little phaeton coming straight at them very fast. He put out one arm to prevent Margaret being thrown forward against the splash-board. The little carriage missed them by inches, and Margaret saw that it was Lady Selina driving it.

The marquis reined in his horses, his face thunderous.

'That is the outside of enough!' he

exclaimed furiously, turning to look at Lady Selina who made no effort to stop. 'If she can not control her cattle, she should stick to donkey-carts!' He turned to Margaret. 'Are you all right, Miss Lambart?' he asked anxiously.

'Yes, I thank you, sir!' Margaret replied rather shakily.

The marquis turned round to his tiger.

'You all right, Hawkins?'

'Yers, my lord. Caw, that were a close 'un, m'lord!'

The marquis's mouth tightened, and he straightened his horses and they set off again at a walk.

'I must apologise to you yet again, Miss Lambart. It seems I am continualy having to apologise to you for some — unfortunate action on the part of my kin! I really cannot think what Lady Selina was about!'

'Lady Selina is fond of fast driving,' Margaret murmured, still a little shaken.

'*Wild, I* should say,' responded the marquis with some acerbity. 'I shall speak to Oxford; he really should keep his sister under better control. He is far too easy with her.'

* * *

Margaret drove in the park again that week with Lord St George, and found the experience totally agreeable. This time Lady Selina was seen only in the distance. Of the Duke of Oxford there was still no sign.

To Margaret's intense surprise one morning, Lady Selina came to Hanover Square and asked to see her. Wondering what Lady Selina could possibly have to say to her, she told Joshua to show her in and greeted her visitor composedly.

Lady Selina was all charm and smiles.

'It is kind in you to receive me, Miss Lambart,' Lady Selina said in a soft voice that Margaret had not heard before. 'I had meant to call upon you earlier to apologise for our little contretemps the other day, but I have been so busy . . . But I was so surprised to see you with St George, my attention was quite taken from my driving for a moment. I had thought — you and St George — but I am glad to see that all is now well between you . . .'

And Lady Selina smiled quite engagingly.

'Oh, yes,' Margaret said calmly; 'we understand one another very well now.'

She was not at all sure whether her visitor was apologising for nearly upsetting her the other day, or for the earlier scene. But her breath was quite taken away by Lady Selina's next words.

'I am afraid that we have not always understood each other as well as we should have done. I regret my — my own part.'

And the girl smiled again.

Margaret was thunderstruck. She wondered at first if she had misheard, but no; Lady Selina was smiling still.

Margaret determined to be generous in her reply.

'I — I fear some of the blame must lie with me, ma'am. A stranger, entering in to an established set, should always endeavour to make their intentions plain. I regret that I was at fault in this!'

Lady Selina gave a small bow and looked at a chair. Margaret invited her to seat herself which she did.

'I — I am exceedingly fond of my aunt, you know, Miss Lambart. My aunt's welfare has always been a most particular concern of mine.'

'I think you will find that Lady James is in the best of spirits, ma'am.'

'Oh, indeed she is! I confess I have not seen my dear aunt near so cheerful this age!'

'I am so glad you think so.'

There was a little pause during which the two women smiled at each other. Then both spoke together and apologised.

'I was only about to enquire how

you had been enjoying the season, Miss Lambart,' Lady Selina said when sufficient courtesies on both sides had been displayed. 'You have had a quite remarkable success! Almost the rage indeed!'

'Oh, Lady Selina!' Margaret protested, not quite sure how to take the remark; 'Surely Miss Philips occupies that eminence!'

'But *you* are such a convenient height, ma'am!' Lady Selina said blandly; 'you must find it a great advantage in a crowd. I hate little dumpy women. Miss Philips is an agreeable enough girl, it is true, but I must confess that I find this season's females a great deal less outstanding than those of previous years.'

Margaret stared at the girl, not at all certain whether she was being complimented or not. Lady Selina's voice went bubbling on.

'I am so glad you are finding the season agreeable, ma'am. Do you know, Miss Lambart, I almost envy you, seeing it all for the first time! The balls, the concerts, the theatres, the parties — there really is nothing to compare with them in the country. They are all so provincial after one has experienced the London season. I am sure you will find it so! Ah, yes!' And Lady Selina smiled reminiscently. 'Do you know, Miss Lambart, this is my third — no! — fourth season! It hardly seems possible, does it?'

'Er — no, indeed, ma'am,' Margaret murmured, wondering what would come next, and perfectly aware that this was Lady Selina's sixth if not seventh season.

'But it is, dear Miss Lambart! I remember so well, though, how timid I felt at my first ball! I could hardly bring myself to say a word; quite the little mouse! But now! Do you know, ma'am, I vow I feel quite *jaded*. But then one must do one's duty, must one not? I mean, when one is *in* society, one must play one's part, must one not? After all it would not do to leave

257

society to those — less well qualified, shall we say? One has seen what has happened at Bath. The Rooms — quite taken over by people one would not at all wish to know. It had to stop, of course; positively it had to stop!'

'I am afraid I am not acquainted with Bath, ma'am,' Margaret said, wondering where the conversation was leading.

'*Anybody* goes now, Miss Lambart! Absolutely anybody! And so of course, one only goes to private entertainments. For a time, of course, one might find oneself presented to anyone at a ball, and that of course, had to stop! I remember Lady Pentreath telling me that she knew of the daughter of a totally obscure country clergyman being presented to the son of a very rich and old-established Gloucestershire family. Certainly, he was a second son, and was indeed, in Holy Orders himself. The master of ceremonies did not presume to present this female to the elder son. But although it happened some years ago, I vow I felt quite upset when I learnt that the creature and the second son were, eventually, married! The young man's father, a General, was greatly distressed, and I am not surprised. He was *very* rich and had a fine old abbey in the country: quite a famous one, I believe, though I have not seen it myself. I do so abhor these mésalliances, do not you, Miss Lambart?'

'I really do not think that I — '

Lady Selina leaned forward and whispered,

'I remember the scandal when Lord Peter Fulwood married Miss Witheringham, the comedy actress. She was exceedingly pretty, of course, and Lord Peter was only the second son, but they quickly found someone willing to be *Lady* Fulwood, for all that Lord Fulwood was not quite right in the head. Miss Witheringham *drank*, you see! Poor Lord Peter! He could not bear the shame. He is in the Peninsula now with Moore, I collect.

But really, he had no one but himself to blame!'

'I always dislike to hear of unhappy marriages,' Margaret said. 'But too many people, I fear, marry for the wrong reasons.'

'Oh, how I agree with you, Miss Lambart! Affection, of course, is necessary — '

'Of course.'

'But so much more is needed if the union is to be a truly happy one: the approbation of one's family and friends; unity of interests and background; a comparability of position and wealth — '

Lady Selina paused, and gave Margaret a searching glance.

'Certainly,' Margaret replied, 'the partners in a union with all these advantages, would be unfortunate indeed, were it to fail.'

'That is why I feel so fortunate, Miss Lambart,' Lady Selina said confidentially. 'I have, of course, had many other offers, — some from the very foremost Corinthians — but . . . '

Lady Selina paused then leant forward and said in a whisper,

'I have had always an understanding with one who is so eminently suitable in every way. Our families have long wished it — for we are quite on a par — everything indeed could not be more favourable: rank, position, fortune . . . '

Lady Selina looked at her meaningfully.

'I know you will understand me, Miss Lambart.' She smiled coyly. 'I know that I can depend upon your discretion . . . '

'You mean,' Margaret exclaimed, quite unaccountably experiencing a sudden sinking feeling, 'that you and — and your kinsman are . . . '?

Lady Selina blushed prettily and bent her head.

'Please — permit me to offer you my most sincere felicitations, ma'am,' Margaret managed to say quite calmly, though she was in turmoil inside.

Her mind darted back to the time

when she had thought Lady Selina and Lord St George well matched; now, she was not near so sure. In fact, she doubted it very much. Not to put too fine a point upon it, she was quite certain that Lady Selina would not suit the marquis at all!

'It — it is all, of course, a great secret,' Lady Selina said confidentially. 'Nothing is to be said yet, but — before very long . . . before the end of the season . . . '

Margaret fought to keep calm. Was not it strange that the marquis should ask her to drive out with him if all the time he were betrothed, albeit secretly, to another woman? For Margaret had no doubt that it was to Lord St George that Lady Selina was referring. But — a long-standing understanding — it was all too possible.

Margaret sighed, and endeavoured to make a suitable reply. She was thankful that Lady Selina took her departure shortly after this.

When she was alone, she endeavoured

to come to terms with this new situation. But — what new situation? After all, nothing was changed. From the beginning she had assumed that Lady Selina and the marquis had an understanding; why should she feel so overset now that she had been told plainly that it was so? She really had no business feeling so . . . so . . .

She was still not yet herself when the footman came to announce the arrival of Lord St George himself. Inwardly, Margaret felt quite flustered, but made a creditable determination to grasp the nettle without delay. She asked for his lordship to be shown up.

She smoothed down her dress, and waited for the sound of feet ascending the staircase: her outward composure quite at variance with her inward feelings.

'Lord St George! What a very pleasant surprise! I had not expected to see you today, sir. I am afraid you have just missed Lady Selina.'

The marquis bowed, and looked a little surprised.

'I had not thought to see her here, ma'am.'

'Oh, but I thought that you must . . .' Margaret began.

She must get it done now, she decided. She smiled as composedly as she could manage and held out her hand.

'Permit me to offer you my felicitations, my lord. I — hope you will be very happy.'

The marquis now looked totally astonished.

'You are very kind, ma'am, but I cannot think why I should deserve them.'

Margaret tried to repress a blush.

'I — must beg your pardon, sir. I know that — it is not yet public property, but Lady Selina was so kind as to confide in me . . .'

'Just what did Lady Selina confide, Miss Lambart?'

Margaret felt more dismayed than ever. Really Lord St George's countenance looked quite thunderous.

'The — the news of your betrothal, my lord,' Margaret faltered.

'My betrothal!'

Margaret nodded.

'Yes. Lady Selina has just told me — '

'Then Lady Selina has quite misinformed you, ma'am! I am certainly not betrothed to anybody!'

Margaret stared at Lord St George, her heart jumping about quite out of its usual place. It was really no concern of hers, but — she did feel inordinately glad that the marquis was not betrothed after all. A broad smile spread over her face.

'Are you quite sure, sir?'

'I most certainly am, Miss Lambart!'

Now the marquis himself broke into a smile.

'I most certainly am!' he repeated.

'H — how stupid of me! I must have quite misunderstood Lady Selina!'

'I wonder what she was about?' Lord St George mused.

'Lady Selina herself may be betrothed and — and I did not clearly comprehend . . . '

'I suppose she told you it was a great secret?' the marquis suddenly demanded.

'Yes. But — understood . . . '

'Well, I have heard nothing of Selina's betrothal!' the marquis said grimly. 'I shall certainly go to her to find out — '

'Oh, pray, sir, do no such thing! Lady Selina will be very vexed with me; I should not have mentioned it . . . '

'But I am extremely glad that you did, ma'am. However, none of this is to the purpose.'

Margaret looked questioningly at Lord St George.

'Some friends and I have arranged an excursion to Kew, Miss Lambart, to see the gardens. I would be very honoured if you would accompany me, ma'am. My sister and Grampian are to be of the party, and I think we should have a pleasant time.'

'Thank you, sir!' Margaret cried, her eyes shining, and feeling quite extraordinarily happy. 'I should like that of all things!'

9

The season progressed on its predestined way, and the day of Margaret's presentation at the Drawing-Room drew closer, and Lady James and Hannah grew daily more excited over the preparations. Margaret herself enjoyed the days of high summer. Major Brummell called at Hanover Square at least twice a week; she made two firm friends in the Duchess of Berrington and Lady Grampian; and her quarrel with Lord St George — or rather, his quarrel with her, was a thing of the past, and he would frequently invite her to drive with him in the park at the fashionable hour. Of the Duke of Oxford and his sister she saw nothing.

Margaret had not realized how quickly the pleasant peaceful days were slipping by till the departure of Major Brummell brought home to her how short would be the time left to her in the capital.

'His Royal Highness wishes to go to Brighthelmstone, Miss Lambart, and I must accompany him. But I look forward to seeing you again upon my return.'

'I — I fear I shall not be here then, sir,' Margaret said, feeling suddenly melancholy.

'Not here! What do you mean, ma'am?'

'I must find some situation, sir — as a companion. That has always been my intention.'

'Never! You cannot do that, Miss Lambart!'

Major Brummell's horrified look and vehement tones made Margaret smile.

'But I cannot stay with my godmother indefinitely, sir.' Now Margaret could not help laughing as she saw the expression on her companion's face. 'Oh, Major Brummell! It really is quite agreeable in the country, you know!'

'*I* have never found it so, ma'am,' Major Brummell replied sombrely. Then he looked at Margaret severely. 'You have done very wrong not to accept one of those offers you have received, Miss Lambart!' He looked at her through his glass. 'You have been exceedingly improvident!'

'I really cannot think what you mean, sir!' Margaret said uncomfortaby. 'I am hardly likely to have had a great many offers. Consider my age and situation — '

'Miss Lambart!' Major Brummell spoke so severely that Margaret broke off at once. 'I have had occasion to speak to you of it before, and I really do wish you would follow my advice. There really is *no* need to point out so continually that you are — somewhat older than most young women making their debut. Only grandparents are permitted to boast of their age!'

Margaret laughed uncertainly.

'But — it is a fact which influences me considerably — '

'Then it must not! You make everyone think you should be retired to a sofa by the fire and wearing your cap!'

'I — threw away my caps when I set out for London, sir,' Margaret said, still not quite herself.

'I am very glad to hear it! Were I a marrying man, I should be on my knees before you this very moment! *Then* we should hear no more nonsense about age and companions!'

'Then I am very glad you are not, sir,' Margaret returned with a stronger laugh, 'for I should certainly have to refuse you, and I should not at all like to do that!'

Major Brummell bowed.

'I have one great regret, ma'am, at leaving London now, and that is that I shall not see you at the Drawing-Room.'

'Oh, sir! I had not thought of that! And I had been depending upon you to support me; I feel so very nervous.'

'There is no need for that, Miss

Lambart,' Major Brummell said roundly. 'All you have to do is think how His Majesty might look without his crown and in his sleeping cap, and I guarantee you will not feel nervous a moment longer!'

'Oh, for shame, sir!' Margaret laughed. 'You are impossible!'

And then to Margaret's regret, she had to take her leave of Major Brummell, for the court-dressmaker appeared for a fitting for the old-fashioned gown it was still necessary to wear to meet Their Majesties.

★ ★ ★

But if Margaret lost one friend in the morning, that very evening she made a new one who was destined to play a great part in her life.

The Earl of Frampton was a widower, and Margaret met him at the card party that evening at Lady Delany's. He was a tall, distinguished-looking figure with a face, not exactly handsome, but very agreeable, with greying hair and an attractive smile. He was adept at cards, and with him as a partner, Margaret could do no wrong. They won all their games together, and when they were parted, the earl said with a bow that he wished that all his partners brought him such luck.

It was when the tea-tray was brought in that the earl sought her out again, and then Margaret learnt that he was the father of four small children. It was but natural that they should compare notes on the upbringing of children without a partner.

'I think I was lucky, sir! I had no brother, and I suspect that girls are easier to handle than young boys — at least, it seems so from what I have seen of my nephews.'

'Ah, there we have the rub, ma'am, for to me it is the girls who present the problem. I am quite unable to see inside their minds, and suspect that I am either too lenient or too harsh. I know that they can twist me round their little fingers if they wish. With my son, I can take him riding or shooting or fishing — but the girls — I fear they are sadly in need of a mother, ma'am.'

The earl begged permission to wait upon Margaret in Hanover Square, which she duly gave. Lord Frampton presented himself the very next day as soon as he decently could, and the conversation followed much the same lines as it had the previous evening.

'But, surely a good governess would be the answer to your problems, sir?'

'A *good* governess, perhaps, Miss Lambart, but where is such to be found? Indifferent governesses are to be found very easily, but a good governess — ah? And I fear the children will soon be out of hand.'

'As their father, sir, I am sure you will not find difficulty in remedying this, should it come about.'

The earl shook his head with a fond smile.

'Alas, Miss Lambart, I have not such

faith in my powers.'

Margaret felt that the earl might have made a push to display rather more steel in his character.

'I am sure your children have delightful natures, sir,' she said kindly, 'and only require a little management.'

'They are so like their dear mother, Miss Lambart. When I see them, I confess I have not the heart for it.'

'Oh, sir,' laughed Margaret, hoping to rally him, 'then unless you find a good governess, I am afraid you must submit to being ruled by your children!'

'I very much fear that you are right, Miss Lambart. Unless — ' and here the earl sighed.

The quarter of an hour being now up, he rose and departed, expressing the hope that they would meet again very shortly.

Margaret mentioned her new acquaintance to Lord St George when she drove out with him that aftrnoon. The marquis was not acquainted with

Lord Frampton and remarked that if all he could talk about was his late wife and his unruly brats, Margaret must have had a poor time of it.

The following morning the earl appeared again, early as before. On the third morning, he presented himself again and stayed the full half hour.

Lady James was half coy, half disappointed, when she spoke to Margaret about her visitor.

'My dear — on three successive mornings! And now the half hour! Of course, he must be trying to create for himself a nearer interest.'

'Indeed I am sure you are mistaken, ma'am. I do not suppose he has found many people in London willing to discuss his problems. For most people such conversation can have little interest.'

Her godmother shook her head, and looked at Margaret curiously.

'You mark my words, my dear,' she said wisely, 'he will make you an offer sooner or later.'

Margaret tried to laugh off the idea, but now that it was implanted, she could not quite dislodge it from her mind. Certainly, she acknowledged to herself, it would be a very suitable match, and she would be, after all, well qualified to look after the earl's motherless children. She was, none-the-less rather startled when Lord St George enquired after her new suitor.

'My suitor, sir?'

'Frampton, of course, Miss Lambart. Upon my soul, you are having an amazingly successful season.'

'Oh! You are as bad as Lady James, sir! Lord Frampton is glad to have a sympathetic listener, that is all. I know all his problems, though I must say, I think his lordship would have rather less trouble if he were a little firmer!'

'He sounds a very dull dog to me!' The marquis kept his eyes firmly on the track ahead. 'Surely he must speak sometimes of other things?'

'No, I do not think so,' replied

Margaret after a moment's reflection. 'He is still grieving for his late wife.'

'Humph! Well, Miss Lambart, your situation is a great deal graver than I had supposed. If a man is forever prosing on about his griefs, it is a sure sign that his mind may be easily turned to another object, especially by a fair and sympathetic listener who is always to hand. Do not say I did not warn you!'

'Oh, pray, sir, do not alarm me!' Margaret laughed.

'I do not wish to alarm you, Miss Lambart, but I have heard of such 'inconsolable' cases before, and I would put you upon your guard. Do not be too — sympathetic, or you may find yourself more — committed — than you had meant.'

'Well, I cannot claim to have your experience or insight, sir, but, truly, I think you exaggerate my danger!'

The marquis turned to her abruptly and gave her a searching look, then he resumed his scrutiny of the track ahead.

278

'Shall I see you at the Italian concert this evening, Miss Lambart?'

'Oh, yes, my lord; Lady James and I will both be there. Did not you know that her ladyship is acquainted with the patroness? At least — ' Margaret stopped, and looked a little uncomfortable for the moment. 'I am afraid I must admit to a sad lack of musical appreciation — and knowledge.'

'But I have heard you play upon the pianoforte quite delightfully, Miss Lambart!'

'You are, as always, very kind, sir, but I am uncomfortably aware of the deficiencies in my performance.'

The fact of the matter as regards the concert was that Lady James and Margaret had decided, neither of them much caring for music, to send a subscription to the concert, but not to attend. However, the Earl of Frampton had secured a box, and had invited them both to accompany him, and Lady James had made haste to accept on behalf of them both.

'But, ma'am!' Margaret had exclaimed as soon as the earl had departed. 'I had thought you did not wish to go!'

'But I had thought that *you* did, my dear.'

'*I*!' Margaret looked more astonished than ever. 'But, why, ma'am?'

Lady James looked at her with the coy glance she so often turned on Margaret now.

'You like the earl very well, do not you?'

'Yes, but — '

'Oh, I know that the *cause* is not one close to your heart: the better propagation of the Gospel in the nether parts of the island of Britain hardly beats a drum in my own breast! But — the company, my dear!'

'I suppose it will be quite a brilliant company, ma'am, but you know I do not care for that,' Margaret said, deliberately misunderstanding her godmother.

'I was referring to the earl, my dear,'

Lady James said reproachfully; 'he was so very anxious for your company, I could see, that I could not bear to deprive him of it!'

Margaret looked at Lady James, puzzled; she could not think what her godmother might be about — unless — it was that she wished Margaret to marry the earl, and thought to promote his suit! Margaret had, once or twice lately, broached the subject of looking for a post as a companion now that the season was reaching its end, but Lady James had never been the least enthusiastic for the idea. Now, yes! Surely that must be it! Margaret sighed. It was unfortunate, but she had no heart for it.

During the interval at the concert that evening, Lord St George presented himself at the earl's box and was introduced by Lady James. The marquis then paid Margaret a light compliment on her appearance and turned to the earl.

'You know, Frampton, that you are

the envy of a great many of the company this evening. Miss Lambart will accept so few invitations; to have her in your box is a trophy indeed!'

Margaret blushed, and looked with slight irritation at the marquis. Lord Frampton answered in an assured manner.

'I am quite aware of my good fortune, St George.'

Then the earl turned to smile at Margaret with an almost proprietorial smile.

'You are enjoying the concert, ma'am?' St George said, turning to Margaret.

'Oh, yes, it is very pleasant, I thank you,' Margaret said, aware that the earl was listening.

But at that moment Lady James spoke to Lord Frampton, and St George bent down to Margaret and spoke in a whisper.

'I had collected from what you said earlier, Miss Lambart, that you were to attend the concert from altruistic motives. But now I find the matter is quite otherwise! Pray do not come to me and say that I did not warn you, ma'am!'

'Oh, you are a great deal too bad, sir!' Margaret whispered back. 'Quite as bad as Lady James! Which is why we are here! But I can assure you, Lord Frampton has no such idea in his mind as you insist on crediting him with!'

The marquis merely answered with a significant smile, and Margaret, feeling quite put out, bent over her programme and studied it minutely. She did wish that her godmother and her nephew would not forever talk of Lord Frampton's intentions. It was almost as if they were pushing her at him!

The interval being over, Lord St George retired, and Lord Frampton seated himself again next to Margaret.

'I suppose you see a great deal of his lordship?' the earl asked.

'He visits my godmother, his aunt, every day,' Margaret whispered, for the music was beginning again.

'Does he indeed!' Lord Frampton replied, not looking at all pleased.

The following morning, the two men met again.

The earl arrived at his usual early time, and close on his heels came Lord St George, a great deal before his usual time. The marquis settled himself comfortably in his chair, and smiled benignly on the other two; the earl looked distinctly put out at his presence.

For the next twenty minutes, Margaret had to work quite hard to keep the conversation afloat; the earl said little and continued looking disgruntled; the marquis said even less, but sat back in his chair and continued to smile blandly.

The marquis won. Being kinsman to the owner of the house, his visit was not confined to a mere half-hour, and so he was able to remain when etiquette constrained the earl to go.

When Lord Frampton was gone, Lord St George looked decidedly smug.

'Really, my lord, you are a great deal too bad!' cried Margaret, not quite certain whether she wished to laugh or scold him.

'But I have done nothing, ma'am!' the marquis said, looking slightly aggrieved.

'You quite put out Lord Frampton!' Margaret retorted.

'On the contrary, I might say, he had put me out. I am come somewhat early for our rehearsal today, for I have an engagement later this morning to go to Tattersall's, and as the Drawing-Room is quite soon, I thought we should not miss our little session. But, clearly, Miss Lambart, as you think I had an ulterior motive in . . . '

The marquis sounded almost offended and Margaret hastily apologised, and hurried to get her hoop. She did not see the smile on his lordship's face as she hastened from the room.

For several days, now, the marquis had been drilling Margaret in her curtsey while wearing a hoop. Unaccustomed to the cumbersome and heavy garment, he had suggested that she should practice wearing it before the Drawing-Room, and often Lady James joined in the rehearsals taking the place of the queen, while his lordship stood in for the king.

'That is very good, Miss Lambart!' the marquis said, when Margaret had curtseyed and walked backwards several times. 'You manage it now as to the manner born!'

'Thank you, sir!'

For some reason Margaret felt as pleased as a child who has unexpectedly been given a lollipop.

* * *

The Earl of Frampton continued to visit Hanover Square. In fact, he was doggedly assiduous in his attentions, and Margaret had to agree with her godmother that he did indeed seem to be making her his object.

The odd thing was that, as Margaret

came to consider the matter with some seriousness, Lady James grew clearly less enthusiastic and even began to hint at the disadvantage of such a match. As Margaret thought that the assurance of a comfortable home and a dignified position in society had a great deal to be said for them, Lady James began to mention the disparity in their ages, and the inconveniences which could ensue from taking on a ready-made but unseen family. Lord St George continued in his original opinion that the earl was a dull dog, and that Margaret should be careful.

'Just imagine, Miss Lambart, it seems that now Frampton has only one topic of conversation, his children; I venture to suggest that when they are your step-children, you might find them a tedious topic every evening as you sit companionably together in your slippers in front of the fire. For he believes that wives should stay at home, you remember! I fear you will not have much society up there in Worcestershire or wherever it is!'

'You forget, sir,' Margaret laughed, 'that I have only been used to society for one season.'

Nevertheless, his remarks did make her think. It would be very much like being at home again with her four younger sisters.

But the day of the Drawing-Room rapidly approached and preparations for it for a while drove her perplexities about the earl from her mind. In any case, he had not as yet said anything to the purpose, and until he did . . .

On the day itself Margaret was dressed in plenty of time to be ready when Lord St George should call for Lady James and herself. Thanks to the rehearsals with the marquis, she was adept at managing her hoop, and had no fear of making what her godmother described as a 'cake of herself'.

'Hoops were a great deal wider when I was a girl, my dear. There was nothing for it but to go sideways through a door, and I remember Lady

Dartingdale getting stuck at Court, once. Certainly, she was rather fat, and she tried to sweep straight through with most unfortunate results. It took three gentlemen quite some time to extricate her, and the chamberlain was very angry with her, for the king hated to be kept waiting, and she was not invited to Court for a whole year afterwards.'

But now Margaret was arrayed in her hoop and her embroidered petticoat and her trained robe and her powdered wig with seven tall white ostrich plumes attached to her borrowed tiara, and was in plenty of time to eat some beef pie and oyster sauce under Hannah's stern eye.

'For you will have a long wait, Miss, and we don't want you fainting at the King's feet!'

'But Hannah, I am not at all hungry!' Margaret had protested in vain.

'You will be a great deal hungrier before you get before Their Majesties, so eat up now, and no nonsense!'

It was at this juncture that a maid came to say Miss Lambart's family was come and that they were waiting in the salon.

'My family!' cried Margaret, astounded.

'Your three sisters and their husbands,' the maid confirmed.

'But — what can they want? Oh, Hannah! I shall have to go to them! How do I look? Oh, please help me out of this!' And Margaret held out her arms for Hannah to pull off the linen overgown she had put on to eat the pie.

'You look a treat, miss!' Hannah replied as she pulled off the covering. 'There's no need to get into such a taking just because your family's come!'

'No, you are quite right.'

Margaret stared at Hannah for a moment, then stooped to kiss the maid's cheek. 'Thank you for all your help, Hannah. I will try to be a credit to you.'

'Get away with you, miss! Of course

you will,' Hannah said briskly. 'Just remember, go slowly.'

Margaret nodded, then went to go down to the salon. She wondered what it could possibly be that had brought her family to London. No mention of such a journey had been made in letters from any of them. She opened the doors to the salon and stood on the threshold.

She saw seated in a little group, perched on the edge of their chairs, her sister Anne and her husband, Mr Thornton, her sister Sarah and her husband, the Reverend Arthur Temple, and making up the party, her youngest sister Jane with Sir Thomas Pettigrew. She wondered where her brother Milton could be. The group stared at her in silence for a moment as she stood in the doorway. Slowly the gentlemen rose.

Anne was the first to find her voice. 'Margaret?' she exclaimed. Then more sharply, 'Margaret, is that you?'

Margaret was very conscious of her

beaded and embroidered hooped blue dress, and her powdered wig and nodding plumes, obilgatory for an appearance at Court. But as she stared at her sisters, she became once again the surrogate parent and her nervousness left her.

'To be sure it is, Anne!' she replied with a laugh. 'Have I changed so much these last months?'

Margaret came fully into the room and closed the door behind her.

'What on earth are you doing dressed like that?' Anne demanded, her voice still sharp.

Margaret came towards them, and calmly offered her cheek to each of them in turn. How very — provincial, they looked, she thought, with an inward wry smile.

'This is indeed a surprise!' Margaret said, seating herself, and not answering her sister's question. 'Is all well in Cheshire? I hope you have not come with any ill news?'

'Oh, no,' Sarah said, still looking

dazed; 'there — there is nothing wrong at home.'

'I am greatly relieved to hear it,' Margaret said composedly. 'Then to what do I owe the pleasure of this visit? You are come a little late for the season.'

'Jane told us that she had seen you!' Anne now said accusingly.

'But where was this?' Margaret exclaimed. 'If you have been in London, why did not you call?'

'I — I did not have your address, Meg, and when I wrote to my sisters for it, they decided they had better come to see for themselves.' Jane spoke in a voice scarcely above a whisper.

'I see,' Margaret said dryly, looking round at her other sisters.

'When Jane saw you driving in the park,' Anne said in the same accusing voice, 'she could not believe her eyes. She wrote to us at once.'

'But — why did not you greet me?' Margaret asked Jane.

'You — you were busy greeting

293

His — His Royal Highness at the time,' Jane answered, staring at her eldest sister with considerable awe.

'I was — ! Oh, no! It was Major Brummell I know. I have never met the Prince.'

'But — I conclude you are to appear at Court today,' Thomas Pettigrew now said, looking at Margaret's gown and head-dress.

'At Court!' Anne and Sarah almost shrieked together.

Margaret nodded.

'You!' Again the two spoke in unison.

'It is the last Drawing-Room of the season.' Margaret was annoyed to hear her voice sounding a little apologetically.

'Well, Margaret,' her brother-in-law Arthur said in his usual portentous tones, 'all this has come as a very great surprise to us.' He looked at her almost severely. 'I am not at all sure your time would not have been better spent in helping me with my charitable works at home than dissipating your energies in this way!'

'Jane has been saving these for us!' Anne now said angrily, taking a sheaf of newspaper cuttings out of her reticule, and flourishing them under Margaret's nose.

'And what are they?' Margaret enquired, looking at the cuttings calmly. 'Oh, reports of balls and things. Yes, they always fill up a column or two.'

'It says you have been seen with a great many different gentlemen!' Anne went on furiously. 'Who are they?'

'Oh, you may look them up in the Peerage. They are all quite genuine!' Margaret said tartly.

'But *we* do not know them!' Anne continued. 'I always thought you said it was very vulgar to be the subject of gossip!' And she glared at her eldest sister.

'And are you really to be presented today?' Sarah said hurriedly.

'*We* have never been presented at Court,' Anne said jealously. 'I do not see why *you* need be.'

'My godmother wishes it,' Margaret said, a slight hauteur in her voice which her family had not heard before. 'It is quite usual, in her circle.'

'But all these men with whom your name has been linked, Margaret,' began her brother-in-law James, making his first contribution to the conversation.

'Oh, I assure you, brother, they are all very respectable. Lord Frampton, for instance, is a widower — with four young children — '

'A widower!' exclaimed Sarah. 'That sounds promising, Margaret! Has he made you his object?'

'He has not made me an offer, if that is what you mean,' Margaret replied, suddenly disliking part of her family very much indeed.

'You play your cards carefully, then, I advise you, sister,' said James heavily; 'it would be a match far above what you might expect.'

'Oh, yes, James; indeed, you are quite right,' said Margaret naughtily.

'I did decide a duchess was too high, and so I refused that, but an earl, perhaps, — '

'A duchess!' Anne gasped. 'Do you mean to say you could have been a duchess?' For the first time since she had arrived, all sign of bad-temper had vanished from her face, and there was only astonishment and a certain respect evident.

Margaret nodded without the ghost of a smile.

'I thought it best to refuse,' she said sagely.

'But — did not you think that we might — I mean, it would have been something for us to have a duchess in the family,' Sarah said breathlessly.

'I am afraid I did not think of that at the time,' Margaret murmured apologetically.

'Well, you take Thornton's advice, Margaret,' Arthur Temple now said, and play your cards well with this — er Frampton. You will not get many offers, I daresay.'

'*And* a widower! You would not have to bother with providing an heir, which I daresay you would not like,' Sarah put in. 'You would not expect too much from a widower, and he need not expect too much from you. He is not very rich, I daresay?'

'I have not yet had his lordship's affairs investigated,' Margaret returned drily.

'By jove, sister!' exclaimed James Thornton, 'I never expected to hear you make such a practical suggestion. Very wise! You do that before you commit yourself. Some of these lords can be very behindhand with the world, I am told. If you need help . . . '

Margaret could but stare at him, much too astonished to speak for the moment.

In fact, no one spoke. Margaret hoped for the summons to leave. Sir Thomas looked embarrassed, while his wife regarded her eldest sister with some awe. Anne and Sarah still stared at her unbelievingly, while the other two men still nodded their heads importantly over this last piece of practical advice. Sarah found her voice first.

'I have been wondering, Margaret, about your jewels. Are they paste? I know you have no such pieces of your own.'

'Of course they are paste!' Anne said crossly.

'I assure you, they are not!' Margaret said, indignation over-coming her astonishment. 'Every one is genuine!'

'Then where did you get — ?' Anne began.

But to Margaret's relief the door opened and Joshua stood in the doorway.

'My lady and his lordship are downstairs, Miss. His lordship says as it's now time to depart, Miss.'

'Thank you, Joshua. Pray tell her ladyship and his lordship that I will be down directly.'

Thankfully, Margaret rose and surveyed the assembled members of her family.

'I must beg you to excuse me now. I dare say I shall see you again while you are in London?'

She offered her cheek again for each of them to peck in turn.

'We are depending upon you to show us fashionable London,' Anne said sharply. 'There is no point in having you here if we do not get any advantage out of it!'

'No. I suppose not,' Margaret murmured, standing very straight, her wig and plumes making her seem to be towering over them all. Then without another word, she swept from the room, her silken train rustling over the carpet, and her feathers barely clearing the top of the door-frame.

Slowly she descended the staircase. Below she saw Lady James, in hoop dress and with befeathered head, seated in the only armchair; beside her stood Lord St George, in a brocade coat and white satin knee-breeches, his dark hair covered by a neat powdered wig, his hand resting upon his sword hilt. On his breast glittered a diamond star. Both of them watched Margaret as she moved down to them.

As she neared the last step, the marquis moved forward, and taking her hand, he lifted it to his lips. He did not say anything for a moment, but admiration was writ very plain in his eyes. Margaret felt her heart miss a beat as she looked at him. No one had ever looked at her in that way before.

Lady James had no difficulty in expressing herself.

'Margaret, my dear, you look radiant. Why, even Emma did not look better in her court-dress, did she, St George? But come, it is time for us to start.' Lady James rose with an effort from her chair. 'I had quite forgot that hoops were so heavy!'

'Oh,' Margaret now exclaimed, 'I have forgotten my fan! I must have left it in the salon. I will just run and fetch it.'

'Indeed you will not, my dear Miss Lambart,' Lord St George said in a whisper, placing one hand upon her arm. 'Joshua will go for it. You really are a great deal too independent. It really will not do, you know.'

And with a slight motion of his head, he indicated Margaret's family, all watching her from the top of the stairs.

Margaret bit her lip and suppressed a giggle.

'I am very sorry, sir,' she whispered back; 'I really will try to improve.'

The fan being restored to her, Joshua opened the door, and the three of them moved out to the carriage. Margaret was very conscious of six pairs of eyes boring into her back.

As Hannah had warned, it was quite impossible for her to sit upright in the coach, for the feathers brushed against the roof, and she had to sit with hunched shoulders to avoid breaking them.

'If only they could have gone in the sword-case as usual,' she sighed.

'I have known ladies sit on the floor

of the coach before today,' Lady James remarked, more happily seated than Margaret being shorter of stature.

'I hardly think Miss Lambart would like that all the way to the palace,' Lord St George remarked.

He was seated opposite Margaret, and if Margaret were not to be discourteous she would have to gaze at his lordship for the greater part of the journey. Self-consciousness was not normally one of her traits, but on this occasion, she experienced it to a considerable degree, and at times it was all she could do to meet his lordship's eyes without faltering.

The marquis himself seemed to talk less than was his wont, and of the three of them, only Lady James herself seemed as usual. Margaret put down the tingling feeling she experienced, a feeling quite foreign to her, as being due to apprehension at what was awaiting her.

But once they were entered the palace, she felt more herself. She leaned gratefully upon Lord St George's arm, and almost before she was aware of it, she had made her obeisances to His Majesty, and to the Queen, to one Prince and to three Princesses. She did not trip over her hoop, nor did her feathers fall off, and then she was out of the Presence, and was being offered wine and cakes by a flunkey. It was then she had time to look about her, and to realize that what had been in the planning for weeks was now all over.

'Well, Miss Lambart, and how did you find it all?' Lord St George asked, smiling. 'I must congratulate you upon your deportment; no one would have guessed you had not performed the ceremony a dozen times at least.'

'Thank you, sir. But any grace I may have shown was entirely due to your tuition. I cannot think how I should have managed had not you made me rehearse.'

'I should have recommended a dancing master to my aunt,' Lord

St George whispered. 'But I enjoyed my role as tutor.'

'It would not have been near so agreeable, sir,' Margaret said with a smile.

Lord St George was about to say something when the Earl of Frampton appeared suddenly at Margaret's elbow. She was surprised to see him, and acknowledged that he made a handsome figure in a green velvet coat embroidered with silver thread. Not as handsome as the marquis, though.

'Lady James, your servant, ma'am,' the earl said, bowing. 'Miss Lambart, you were magnificent. Permit me to congratulate you. I felt very proud when I saw you.'

And he took Margaret's hand and carried it to his lips.

'Thank you, sir,' Margaret said politely, recovering her hand as soon as she could.

Lord St George, however, seemed to have lost something of his usual urbanity.

'In*deed*!' he said frostily, peering at the earl through his glass. 'You felt *proud* of Miss Lambart, did you sir?'

'I — I meant,' said the earl, a little confused by this plainly rather hostile scrutiny, 'that I am proud to count such a beautiful creature among my — my friends.'

The earl finished with some firmness, and fingered his own glass.

'You find Miss Lambart beautiful?' the marquis demanded coldly.

'Indeed I do, sir!' the earl replied with some warmth.

Margaret wondered with some amusement how long they might stand there quizzing each other. Suddenly the marquis's manner changed.

'You must miss your late wife on such occasions as these, sir,' he said sympathetically. 'Doubtless they conjure up a myriad melancholy thoughts.'

'When one has known perfection, sir, its loss must always oppress; but tonight I feel no particularly nostalgic sentiments, for my wife was not at Court above twice. She preferred to concern herself, I am happy to say, with her duties in the home.'

'Doubtess you also preferred to see her so occupied, sir?' the marquis remarked with a bland smile.

'Certainly, sir, I think it is a woman's duty to keep more to the domestic side of life. I do not care to hear women talk of politics, they have no sense in such things. Some of these so-called — intellectual women — ' and the earl put a quantity of scathing into the word, 'are, in short, entirely unwomanly, sir. No, no; if a woman is to fulfil her proper role in life, as did my late wife — to perfection, sir, — then there will be little time for the — fripperies of the London season.'

The marquis raised an eyebrow.

'Oh, come, sir!' he expostulated mildly. 'Fripperies! Is not a little pleasure permissible for a few short weeks in the year?'

'Oh, it may, perhaps, be allowable

if the domestic duties permit it; if the children should have no need of their mother's guiding hand. But I am very happy to say that the late countess had no wish to pass her time here in London. She much preferred to remain at our country seat, keeping my mother company, and attending to the needs of her helpless children.'

And the earl looked sentimentally as he said this.

The marquis murmured, 'She sounds a very paragon, sir,' and turned towards Margaret, smiling blandly.

'She was, sir; indeed she was,' the earl replied.

'But *you* come to London frequently, sir? I wonder I have not before had the pleasure of making your acquaintance?'

'Oh, that is not to be wondered at, sir; I am very little in the capital. I prefer Bath.'

'Ah.' The marquis nodded his head wisely.

'The waters, you know; they suit me.'

'I see,' the marquis said sympathetically, and nodded wisely again.

'I have tried the waters at Cheltenham, sir, but I regret to say that they did not suit me at all. And, of course, I like to meet my old friends, and so I am faithful to Bath. Of course, it is not what it was when I was younger, but — if one's constitution will not be satisfied elsewhere . . . ' And the earl shrugged expressively.

'You suffer much, sir?' the marquis asked, all sympathy.

For answer the earl looked heavenwards.

'Beyond description, sir!' he said after a moment.

'And in addition to these troubles, you have four children I collect, sir! A heavy burden to bear alone.'

'Indeed it is, my lord!'

The earl nodded his head lugubriously.

'But you have, perhaps, been fortunate in finding a suitable governess, sir?' the marquis went on, more bracingly.

'Alas, no, sir.' The earl continued

to look mournful. 'I have, indeed, taken into my employ a female in that capacity, but, as to suitable — ! Besides, my lord, a governess can not fulfil all the duties of a wife!'

'Just so, sir!' the marquis agreed hastily. 'Er — entertaining your guests, and so on.' The marquis waved a vague hand and gave a sympathetic smile. 'And so, now you come to London to — er — ?'

The earl cast a quick glance at Margaret, saw that her attention was engaged elsewhere, then bent confidentially towards the marquis.

'That was indeed my intention, my lord; and I think I may congratulate myself — ' The earl did not finish his sentence but nodded and smiled and looked very pleased with himself.

'Indeed!'

The marquis smiled back in the same fatuous way, tapped the earl knowingly with his glass, and said in a whisper, 'You lucky dog, you!'

Although her attention was called

elsewhere by Lady James, Margaret had in fact heard a good deal of what was passing between the two men. On occasion she felt very strongly that the marquis was roasting the earl; at other times she was somewhat taken aback by the pomposity manifested by the earl. She wondered she had not noticed it before! Previously she had pitied him wholeheartedly for his bereavement, but it did seem now that the late Lady Frampton must have had to endure a decidedly circumscribed and dull life.

On the homeward journey she felt that Lord St George was looking strangely pleased with himself.

'Well, I think we may count that a very successful evening in more ways than one!' he announced in a whisper, so as not to wake Lady James, sleeping in her corner.

'How do you mean, sir?' Margaret whispered back, made suspicious by his tone.

The marquis did not answer at once,

but Margaret could see that he was smiling to himself as the light from the coach head-lamps showed up his face.

'I was anxious to get to know Lord Frampton better, ma'am. I know he is a very particular friend of yours. And as my aunt's god-daughter, I do feel some sense of responsibility for you — as you have no brothers of your own to perform the office for you!'

'What office?' Margaret asked in her normal voice.

'Sssh!' the marquis said with a glance at Lady James.

'What office?' Margaret now hissed.

Really, it was all exceedingly difficult. Lord St George was able to sit quite at his ease, and Margaret felt at a considerable disadvantage, half-crouched as she was because of her feathers.

'The office of enquiring into a suitor's circumstances and intentions, ma'am,' the marquis replied blandly.

'Circumstances and inten — !' Margaret gasped, astounded. 'Well, it is very kind of you, sir, to take so much trouble on my account, but I assure you it is quite unnecessary!' she continued with some heat. 'I may be unprotected, but I am not green, sir!'

'Oh, Miss Lambart!' the marquis said with injured reproof. 'I had only your good in mind. I thought it would be advantageous to find out just what would be expected of you!'

'Nothing is expected of me, sir!' Margaret flashed, feeling suddenly cross.

'If you marry Frampton, there will be.' The marquis smiled blandly. 'Just as there would be, dear Miss Lambart, were you to marry — anybody.'

'I have said repeatedly, sir, that I do not wish — do not intend to be married!'

'I know. And I have always thought it exceedingly strange. I really cannot see you passing your life as a companion, ma'am.'

'Oh, you are quite impossible, sir!' Margaret hissed. She flung up her head, felt her feathers pushing against the roof of the coach, and slumped down to accommodate them once more. She glared at the marquis but the effect of her look was quite lost as the light did not shine on her face.

Her annoyance left her abruptly and was succeeded by a feeling of melancholy, for which she could not account at all. It was, after all, exceedingly kind in the marquis to be concerned for her, but she would much prefer that he did not bother. And when she reached her room and found that the tip of one of her feathers was broken after all, and was hanging down in a very idiotish way, she felt that it was positively the last straw, and she worried Hannah immensely by bursting into tears as she was being undressed.

10

A night's sleep did little to disperse Margaret's despondency, but she endeavoured to appear as usual when she went to greet her godmother. Lady James seemed to be bubbling over with some excitement, but offered no explanation for her condition. The two of them were still talking over the previous day's events when the Earl of Frampton was announced.

'Faith, but the wretched man will be here for breakfast soon!' her ladyship exclaimed.

'But ma'am,' exclaimed Margaret, getting up to go, 'a short time ago you were only too anxious to receive him here!'

'I have changed my mind about him!' her ladyship said loftily. 'Do not let him keep you too long, my dear. I thought we might go shopping

315

together this morning.'

Margaret stared in astonishment. It was very unlike Lady James to venture forth early in the day.

'Of course, ma'am,' she hastened to say.

'And I have one or two calls to make.'

'I will be ready, ma'am.'

But she was not to dispose of the earl quite as quickly as she had expected. She thought he looked rather flushed and restless, but he started off normally enough, asking how she had enjoyed the previous day.

'I enjoyed it very well, sir, I thank you. It was a great experience for me.'

'Indeed it was, Miss Lambart,' the earl replied sententiously.

'I was so afraid I might make some *faux pas* — some terrible mistake. But happily it was all a great deal easier than I had thought.'

'Oh, there was no cause for concern on that score, Miss Lambart; His

Majesty is always very gracious. He would have been certain to overlook any little slip you might have made.'

Normally Margaret liked plain speaking, but in her present mood she did not feel too pleased. She would rather have liked a compliment. After all, she had performed the ceremony with grace, and had not once lost control of her hoops, thanks to the marquis's rehearsals. She had curtseyed to exactly the required depth, had taken the precise number of steps backwards that protocol required on every occasion, without tripping over her train, and had stayed in conversation with each of the Royal Personages for exactly the correct number of seconds. Yes! She might indeed have expected a compliment.

But all she said was, 'I am sure you are right, sir.'

'You — er — have been acquainted with Lord St George a long time, ma'am?' was the earl's next surprising remark.

'Oh, no, sir! It is the marquis's aunt, the Lady James, whom I have known all my life. His lordship I have known only since I came to London.'

'Indeed! I had thought, perhaps, he stood in some way as — your guardian.'

'My guardian!' Margaret exclaimed, competely astonished.

'Yes,' Lord Frampton replied sententiously. 'I may, of course, have been mistaken, but I received the distinct impression that his lordship had a greater interest than that of a mere acquaintance.'

Margaret did not reply for several seconds. She could hardly think what to say.

'Because — of my connection with his aunt, Lady James, Lord St George — does feel an interest . . . ' Margaret said slowly.

When he came to Hanover Square later in the day, she would certainly speak to the marquis on the subject!

'But he is certainly not my guardian!'

Margaret finished with a good deal of firmness.

'I see,' the earl said slowly, then fell to fidgeting with the fringe of a cushion.

'I suppose you will be returning to your children soon, sir?' Margaret asked brightly, to turn the conversation. 'They will be looking forward to seeing you again, my lord, I have no doubt.'

'I shall indeed, ma'am.'

'As you are so little pleased with their governess, I daresay you are anxious about them.'

'It is indeed a heavy responsibility, Miss Lambart,' the earl said soulfully, 'to support alone — as I do now.'

He looked at Margaret with a glance full of meaning, then continued in a melancholy voice.

'But — one must not give way. One must learn to live again — to gather the remnants of one's life — as *I* have done, Miss Lambart.'

The earl continued to gaze at her with a great quantity of sentiment, but Margaret could only think how strangely pompous he sounded. It really was quite remarkable that she had not noticed it before!

Suddenly the earl attempted to seize her hand, and said with a good deal of warmth,

'*You* have taught me to do that, ma'am!'

'I, sir!' exclaimed Margaret, endeavouring to withdraw her hand from the earl's clasp, and her heart sinking at she knew what must come now. Her godmother and Lord St George had been quite right! They had seen the matter a good deal more clearly than she had done. In fact, she had shut her eyes to it for most of the time, so little did she wish to consider it.

'Yes, ma'am, you. I owe you so much!' the earl cried, clinging on to her hand. 'When — when the countess died, Miss Lambart, I never thought to meet such a creature again — you can imagine, I know, how I felt: the companion and solace of my lonely hours; the mother of my children; my dependence for the future, torn from me, ma'am, in the very bloom of her life! Ah, Miss Lambart, it quite unmans me to think of it now!'

And indeed the earl did look as if he might wipe away a tear or two. Margaret still pulled at her hand, but the earl hung on desperately, and after he had expelled a few shuddering breaths, he was once more enough himself to continue speech.

'What I suffered, ma'am, no man can tell. I bore it all patiently, silently — as befits a man and a Christian. I came to London, ma'am, intent upon finding a good governess — someone to care for my little ones, to give them the love and guidance their mother's sudden and too early departure had deprived them of — I looked, Miss Lambart, but — I looked in vain. To find a companion for my own loneliness, ma'am, I did not think to look. I never expected such to exist — though I should search throughout the world, ma'am!'

Margaret felt rather flustered now. It was quite obvious what must be coming, and she felt as incapable of coping with it as if she were a young girl of sixteen.

'But I have not had to search the world, Miss Lambart!' the earl said triumphantly. 'Hardly had I come to London, ma'am, when I met such a woman — such a paragon. Ah, Miss Lambart, how the gods have showered their blessings upon me! And who is that creature, you may ask? That dear, dear creature!'

He paused dramatically, but Margaret could only stare with the same fascination a rabbit might feel for a stoat.

'It is you, Miss Lambart! It is you!' The earl's voice, which had risen to a great crescendo, suddenly sank to a low throb. He looked at her with eyes full of meaning.

'Yes, Miss Lambart, yourself!' he intoned, as Margaret made no sound. 'My intentions must, I am sure, have been plain to you from the first, ma'am, and — I flatter myself — they have not been wholly unwelcome! Miss Lambart — Margaret — for the sake of my children, I see that my duty is plain before me; for the sake of my peace of mind, that duty is my pleasure. I wish now to do that which I had never thought to contemplate again: I wish to remarry, ma'am; and it is you I wish to take as my wife!'

At this, the earl attempted to put his arms round her, but Margaret managed to avoid this, her hand having at last been freed. She walked away in some agitation.

Unbidden, all the advantages of this union sprang to her mind. But when she looked at the earl, they melted into nothingness. In any case, she had no wish — never had had any wish — to marry. At least, if she did, it would be because such a course was prompted by affection.

'I — I must confess, sir,' she

began, 'that — that I am quite overwhelmed. I had never, I assure you, contemplated such an outcome as this to our acquaintance. You have, sir, taken me completely unawares!'

The earl looked a little piqued.

'Surely, ma'am, you must have noticed — must have realized — that my feelings for you were advancing beyond that of a mere acquaintance?' he said reproachfully.

'Indeed, sir — I — I thought you sought me out because of our somewhat similar situations; because I could understand your problems!'

'That indeed, ma'am, was the beginning of my partiality for you; but it did not long remain so, I assure you. Your own good qualities, Miss Lambart, very soon made their impression upon me, and before long I found myself seeking you out, not merely for the comfort I received from your sympathy, but also for the pleasure I felt in your company.'

'You — you are very kind, sir,'

murmured Margaret.

She wondered frantically how she should word her reply.

'Well, ma'am?' the earl said expectantly, moving a little towards her. 'And what is to be my answer?'

Margaret took a step or two backwards.

'I — I am very conscious, sir, of the great honour you do me. And I must confess that I have found our acquaintanceship very agreeable, but — but — '

And tender-hearted Margaret found great difficulty in uttering the words she wished to say. Speedily she thought back over her acquaintance with the earl. Had she perhaps been too encouraging? Should she have been less accessible? When the young Duke of Oxford had proposed, circumstances were quite different. Then such a match was clearly impossible; now, the world would have applauded, and Margaret sought for words to lessen the harshness of the blow she must inflict, and which the earl had perhaps every right not to expect.

But at that very moment, Joshua came into the room with the message that Lady James was ready to set out and would Miss Lambart be long?

When they were alone again, the earl looked decidedly put out.

'I beg your pardon, sir,' Margaret said hurriedly, 'but I must attend Lady James. Could you — would you — allow me a little time in which to think over your proposal? The happiness of so many people depends upon my answer; not only ourselves are concerned, my lord, but also your children. Allow me a few days in which to think, I beg you, sir!'

'Ah, Miss Lambart . . . I had hoped . . . but I honour your thoughtfulness; your wisdom! I will return in two days', ma'am, and expect then to be made the happiest of men!'

And with that, the earl took his leave.

Margaret hurried to put on her bonnet, then sped to her godmother's room. She found Lady James in the middle of a game of patience, and clearly in no particular hurry to be gone.

'Ah, Margaret, my dear!'

'I received your message, ma'am. I am sorry if I have kept you waiting.'

'Not at all, my dear. Is the earl gone?'

'He took his leave when Joshua brought your message, ma'am.'

'He seemed to remain an unconscionable time today!'

'I — did not notice, ma'am.'

Lady James looked sharply at Margaret at this.

'Did he — did he have anything *particular* to say?'

Margaret tried to answer calmly, but her thoughts were still in turmoil, and it was not long before Lady James had the whole from her.

'And what did you say, my dear?' Lady James asked, her face suddenly puckered. 'How did you answer the earl?'

'He — he is coming back for his answer in two days' time, ma'am.'

'Two days!' Lady James looked relieved.

But she said no more, and began to put her cards together.

'I think we had better be going out now, my dear,' she went on after a moment; 'do you think I should wear my shawl or a spencer?'

The question had not been decided, when Joshua appeared again, this time to announce that Lady Grampian was come.

The marchioness danced into the room looking prettier than ever. She greeted her aunt, then turned to Margaret, her face wreathed in smiles.

'Dearest Miss Lambart! Here I am! I expect you never thought to see me so early!'

And she came up to Margaret with outstretched hands.

'Dear Miss Lambart!' she said

anxiously, peering at Margaret's face. 'Are you quite well?'

'I am, perhaps, a little tired, ma'am, after yesterday . . . .' Margaret murmured.

'Oh, yes, such a success! I have heard such things — ! But I am so *very* glad to see you! Grampian was only too happy to oblige — Oh!'

The girl stopped, and put her hand to her mouth in the childish gesture Margaret had seen often before. She glanced at her aunt, then turned back to Margaret, dimpling.

' . . . to oblige *me*!' she finished, her eyes shining. 'When he knew it was *you* I wished to visit, dear Miss Lambart!'

Lady Grampian gazed at Margaret, then rushed on,

'Oh, Miss Lambart, have we not — I mean — could we not — after all, we have known each other quite a long time now, and — Miss Lambart! Would you please call me Emma, and may I call you Margaret? It seems so — so formal — so silly — especially now . . . '

'I should be delighted, Emma; thank you,' Margaret smiled.

Lady James looked on, delighted.

'Do you know, Grampian was quite astonished that I should wish to pay a call at such an early hour!' Lady Grampian went on. 'I am sure I must be your first caller, am not I?'

'Well, no; I am afraid you are not!'

'You mean — someone has been here before me!'

The girl sounded appalled, and turned to look at her aunt.

'Lord Frampton has been here already this morning!' Lady James said with a meaning look.

'Oh, what will St George say! He will be so very angry with me!' Lady Grampian put her hand to her mouth again, and looked quite alarmed. 'I — I mean, he is always calling me a — a slug-a-bed, and — and I did promise him that I would try to mend my ways!'

'But if Lord Grampian makes no objection, I should not have thought your brother — ' began Margaret.

'Oh, you know what St George is! So domineering! So tyranical! Always he wants his own way! At least — I mean — he is very kind generally — a *very* good, kind man — but — with a sister — you know what it is!'

'I am afraid I do not know, not having a brother.'

'Do not you? Oh! You will find it out very quickly when you are married, I promise you!'

The pretty face took on an expression of alarm.

'Your visitor — the earl — was very early, was not he?'

'Punctual, I should rather say,' Margaret said, trying to summon up a smile.

'He is a — a creature of regular habits, I collect?'

'He will come again in two days' time!' Lady James said now.

'Two days!' said Lady Grampian.

'Oh, that is all right then!' And she beamed at Margaret. 'I have nearly forgot — the reason I came. St George asked me to bring you a note.'

And she held an envelope out to Margaret.

Margaret took it and was about to put it in her reticule to read later when Lady James said,

'Pray read your letter now, Margaret my dear; Emma and I will not mind a bit.'

Margaret broke the seal, conscious that both women were watching her closely.

She found a short note from St George, explaining that he had to make an unexpected journey to his estate in Oxfordshire, and begging her to excuse him as he would not be able to keep their appointment to drive together in the park that evening as they had arranged.

She felt a sharp stab of disappointment, but managed to read the note out loud in a calm voice. Her two listeners exchanged a glance, and Margaret folded the note and put it away, wondering rather disconsolately how long the marquis would be absent.

'I — I hope his lordship has not had bad news?' she asked tentatively.

'Oh, no, I do not think so!' Lady Grampian returned with a broad smile.

Some time later Margaret and her godmother were driving down Bond Street when they saw the Duke of Oxford coming out of a jeweller's. Lady James told her coachman to stop, and the young man crossed the street to greet his aunt. Margaret and the duke had met on several occasions now since his proposal to her, and a pleasant friendship had now been established.

'And how is Miss Allenham, your Grace? Pray give her my good wishes,' Margaret said with a smile, referring to the duke's current object.

'I will indeed, ma'am. And I know that Miss Allenham would send her greetings to you also.'

'I suppose you will be going into Kent soon, David?' Lady James asked.

'Next week, ma'am; Miss Allenham and I will go down together.'

'Well, come to see me before you depart, dear boy. It will be too much, I suppose, to expect to see anything of Selina.'

'Oh, Selina is already departed, ma'am. It was all arranged in a very great hurry yesterday evening, and she is gone down into Oxfordshire with St George this morning. I am to have a very great quantity of things sent after her.'

'Indeed!' Lady James said, looking exceedingly put out.

As for Margaret, she experienced at that moment an emotion she had never thought to endure. She felt, to put it quite plainly, thoroughly jealous of Lady Selina. The sharpness of her feeling startled her, and she had a severe inward struggle for composure.

The rest of the day went by

for Margaret in a wretched manner. Whatever she was doing, her mind constantly returned to visions of Lord St George departing for his country estate with Lady Selina, and that evening she was quite unable to concentrate upon her cards as she should have done. For the very first time, she committed the heinous crime of trumping her partner's ace.

Lady James stared in disbelief, but nobly said nothing. When it happened for the second time, she asked with the slightest tinge of annoyance in her voice,

'Are you quite well, my dear?'

Margaret stared at the four cards on the green baize and blushed scarlet.

But the error served to concentrate her mind and take it off her unhappy broodings.

★ ★ ★

The following day was little better. And she was not helped by the appearance

335

at an early hour of her sisters and their husbands, who at once made it plain that they expected her to show them something of fashionable London.

Anne was the first through the door. 'So there you are, Margaret; we really had expected to see you yesterday! I am sure we waited an hour for you at the very least. We simply could not believe that you were gone out when you knew *we* were in London!'

'I am sorry. Lady James wished me to accompany her shopping.'

'We did not know where to go for anything. Sarah wished to purchase some stockings, and I wanted some trimming for a bonnet, but we saw nothing that might not have been bought cheaper in Chester.'

'I am afraid you will find London expensive. Did you go to Grafton House?'

'We did not know where to find it,' Anne said crossly.

'I like your gown, Margaret,' Jane said timidly. 'You look very — elegant.'

'Thank you, Jane.'

'We have been wondering,' Anne now said, 'how it is you can afford so many gowns, Margaret. You never had so many before. I can not think why you should suddenly want them. The one you wore to Court the other evening cost a pretty penny, I'll be bound! And *seven* feathers in your hair! I know, for I counted them!'

In order to stop this inquisition, Margaret was thankful to go out with her kinsfolk and show them some of the sights of London. She did her best to give them an agreeable time, but there is no doubt that she was often preoccupied with her own thoughts, and she was thankful when she could say goodbye to them. She and Lady James were to go to another card party that evening, and though Anne threw out a great many hints that they would like to be included, Margaret did not heed them.

'We are quite at liberty this evening, Margaret; I really cannot think what we should do!'

'Why do not you go to the theatre? I am sure you would enjoy that!'

'I do not feel like going where where will be crowds. It will be so excessively hot!'

'There will be a concert in the park tonight. It will be agreeably cool there this evening.'

'No; we would prefer to go to some small select gathering.' Anne looked hard at her sister. 'Some *private* party, perhaps.'

'I regret that Lady James is not entertaining this evening,' Margaret said with some relief.

But they left her at last, and she was at liberty to think again before it was time for her to go out with her godmother.

Her thoughts had turned so continually to Lord St George and Lady Selina, that it was with a start that she now remembered that tomorrow was the day Lord Frampton was to come for his answer.

Perversely, Margaret now felt some indecision as to what she should say. At the time, she had had no doubt, but, perhaps it was as well that she had been saved from being hasty. After all, she was being offered an elevated situation, and it was not something she should dismiss lightly. To be a countess would have been considered by the world to be a very respectable situation. And after all, the idea of being a companion was not so agreeable as once she had thought it.

In order to clear her mind, Margaret sat down at her desk, drew out a clean sheet of paper, and proceeded to rule a line down the centre of the page. At the head of the first column she wrote 'For', and on the second 'Contra'. Then meticulously, she made a figure one on the left-hand side, and with great care set a full-stop after it.

After much thought she wrote after the figure one: *I would lead a* useful life, with four young, motherless children in need of care.'

Then she wrote down a figure two.

Against this, after some more deliberation, she wrote: '*I would be assured of a respectable position in life, and would have no further concerns on the score of money.*'

Some further thought resulted, some time later, in a third point being equally slowly and carefully inscribed: '*I have no wish now to be a companion.*'

A great while later there were ten points all set down upon the left-hand side of the paper. The right-hand side was still blank.

Margaret gazed at her list. Surely she could find some valid reason to set down against Lord Frampton's suit!

After some moments' further thought, she penned her first sentence in the right-hand column. Almost of their own accord the words appeared: '*I do not wish to marry Lord Frampton because I love Lord St —*'

Margaret stopped and gazed astonished

at what she had written. Then hastily she scratched it out so that not a single letter could be deciphered. Then she sat back in her chair, panting.

Why had not she realized this before? How could she have been so blind? It would account for so many things: her disappointment when she received his lordship's note; her jealousy when she heard of Lady Selina's departure with the marquis! Why had not she recognized her feelings for what they were then?

But even though she did realize the truth of her feelings at last, she could foresee only sadness ahead. She had no hope that Lord St George could love her, and perhaps after all, it would be better to accept Lord Frampton's suit?

11

After a night spent largely in sleepless tossing, Margaret arose the next morning, tired, dark-eyed and more wretched than ever. During the night hours she had come to examine her heart very closely, and she knew that, loving Lord St George as she did, the idea of union with anyone else was totally abhorrent to her.

No matter what might happen to her in the future, no matter how meagre her prospects might be, it was quite impossible for her to accept the earl while she had such feelings for another man.

How long she had loved the marquis she did not know. Certainly, at the beginning, her feelings for him had been anything but cordial. But as she reviewed the last weeks, she realized how she had come to depend upon the marquis for advice and companionship. Her love had stolen upon her gradually, and whatever its origin may have been, it was not now to be set aside.

She could no longer like the idea of being a companion to some elderly, possibly cantankerous female, but that was preferable to a life of forever wishing one was married to someone else.

When Lord Frampton came, therefore, she would tell him as kindly as possible, that she could not marry him. It need not take long, she thought; if only she had had the presence of mind to do it the other day.

She dressed with particular care, choosing a rose-coloured dress which, she hoped, might reflect a little colour into her drawn face, and very unusually she had Hannah dress her hair twice before she was satisfied. Then she went to bid her godmother good morning.

Lady James looked at her anxiously as she entered the room.

'Are not you feeling well, my dear?'

343

'I am afraid I did not sleep well, ma'am. I am a little tired, still.'

'You should have rested longer today, Margaret!'

The girl shook her head.

'You forget, ma'am; Lord Frampton is to come for his answer today.'

Lady James looked not at all happy.

'Ah, yes; I had forgot.' She added, after a pause, 'You have — er — decided upon your answer, my dear?'

'Yes, ma'am.' Margaret paused a second. 'I — I shall thank the earl, and refuse his offer.'

Lady James looked immensely relieved, then she spoke quickly,

'You — are quite certain, my dear? It is a — a very great position you are refusing.'

'I know, ma'am. But truly I could never marry his lordship. You will remember that I have always said that I do not wish to marry,' she added with a slight smile.

'Oh, as to that, I have never taken

much notice of it,' Lady James said dismissively. 'If the right man were to come along, you would change your mind soon enough, I warrant. But I confess I am glad it is not to be the earl. He is a great deal too — too staid for you.'

'At one time, ma'am, I collect you thought otherwise!'

'That was before I had fully thought over the matter, my dear!' Lady James said promptly.

When she had left her godmother, Margaret went to the library, and sat quietly awaiting the arrival of the earl. For once she blessed his punctuality; all might be over very soon, and then she might be left in peace. She did not attempt to read while she waited, but sat quietly on one of the big leather armchairs, her hands folded in her lap.

The earl came upon the minute.

There was a slight reserve in his manner as he greeted her and waited pointedly.

Margaret told him in the kindest possible terms that she could not be his wife. The earl looked exceedingly surprised and then hurt. He urged her very seriously to change her mind, pointing out the advantages of the union, and the fact that they were so very suitable for each other in point of age, and circumstance and in every other way.

Margaret could only smile and not be moved.

'I shall always be very sensible of the honour you have done me, sir, but indeed I cannot change my mind.'

The earl bowed once more and Margaret rang the bell. Joshua appeared, the earl took a dignified leave and was shown out. It was over.

Now that Lord Frampton was gone, Margaret realized that she was trembling. She had been a great deal more tense during the interview than she had supposed, and now she resumed her seat, panting a little, and endeavouring to regain command of herself.

She felt so very, very tired. She closed her eyes and thought about the summer she had spent in Hanover Square. Never again would she know such pleasures, experience such delights, enjoy the company of such a man as the marquis. Even if she did have to spend the rest of her life carrying shawls for elderly ladies and taking over-fed lapdogs for walks, she would always have these golden memories.

She recollected events as through a haze: so many things she had seen, so many people she had met: the beautiful young duchess of Berrington collapsing in the heat of an art gallery; the shy young Duke of Oxford who had thought to make her his duchess; Major Brummell with his exquisitely white shirt-fronts and his irrepressible quizzing; Almack's, Astley's, the Drawing-Room — and through them all flitted the figure of Lord St George.

She seemed almost to see him standing before her; against the light from the window his figure was as though surrounded by a nimbus — but she knew it was only her own imaginings. The marquis was in Oxfordshire — with Lady Selina — and she had no idea when he would come back — if at all.

'Margaret.'

Someone was speaking her name.

She opened her eyes.

The figure was still there, but now it seemed more substantial. She blinked, and tried to see it more clearly.

The figure held out a hand to her and spoke her name again.

Suddenly Margaret was fully awake, fully conscious, and she knew that it was indeed Lord St George standing before her, smiling. He had no halo round him now; his figure was outlined quite sharply against the window panes. She stared at him for a moment, unbelieving.

'You!' she gasped at last. 'It is you, my lord!'

She half rose from her chair.

'I — I thought I might never see you again!'

And she reached out to take the marquis's outstretched hand.

'Why ever not?' the marquis exclaimed, completely astonished.

She could not say that as he had gone into Oxfordshire with Lady Selina she had assumed . . .

'I — I thought there might have been a carriage accident,' she said hurriedly; 'I thought you might be dead upon the road!'

'Dead upon the — !' the marquis began. 'Upon my soul, Miss Lambart, why should you think that?'

Margaret thought frantically. She must say something — anything —

'Your coach might have overturned, and — and there would be no one by to help you!'

'With two footmen with me . . . I fear you have been reading too many novels, Miss Lambart!'

'I — I never read n-novels, sir!' Margaret whispered, struggling to hold back her sudden tears of relief.

Lord St George held her hand very tightly and looked down at her tenderly.

'And would it have upset you, Miss Lambart, if — if there had been an accident?'

Margaret could only nod.

The marquis seized hold of her other hand and drew her to him.

'Miss Lambart — Margaret — I suppose I may call you Margaret, may not I?'

Margaret nodded again, and her eyes were shining as she looked up into the marquis's face.

'I should like it of all things, my lord,' she whispered, her own face very close to that of Lord St George.

The marquis made a movement to embrace her, but at that exact moment there came a loud peal on the front door bell, and as they were downstairs in the library, it sounded very strident.

Lord St George drew back his head, though he did not loosen his clasp of

Margaret, and said in an irritated voice, 'I suppose that is Frampton!'

'Oh, no, my lord! At least, I think not! Lord Frampton has been here already today.'

'He has been here already!'

'You know how punctual he is!'

'And did he . . . did he . . . what did he want?'

'He came for his answer, my Lord,' Margaret teased.

'His answer!' The marquis looked first furious, then distraught. 'I knew it! I knew it! I knew he was upon the point of making an offer, but I hoped — What did you say?'

'I — thanked the earl for his offer . . . ' Margaret said slowly.

'And — ?'

'I — I told him that it was impossible for me to accept it.'

'Thank God for that!' the marquis exclaimed fervently, and then, before there were any more interruptions, he proceeded to kiss Margaret with very great tenderness.

'I — I protest, sir!' Margaret gasped at last, pulling away a little from his encircling arms. 'What did you think I had said? I would hardly be like to find myself in this situation if I had just accepted another man's hand! I am not so fickle, sir!'

The marquis pulled her to him again.

'I was so afraid I should never see you again, sir,' Margaret whispered. 'Why did you hurry away so into Oxfordshire?'

'To fetch this.'

And the marquis pulled a little blue velvet bag from his pocket and handed it to her.

'What is it, my lord?'

'Undo it and see.'

Obediently Margaret pulled at the thin silk cords until there was space enough for her to insert her finger and thumb. She looked then in surprise into the marquis's face, and he smiled at her.

'Take it out, Margaret.'

She withdrew from the little bag

an old-fashioned gold ring set with a huge diamond surrounded by a circle of smaller ones.

'It — it is very beautiful, sir,' she whispered, blushing and staring at it.

'It belonged to my mother, and before that my grandmother. And before that ... Will *you* wear it, Margaret? It is known in the family as Her Ladyship's ring.'

Margaret looked up into Lord St George's face, her lips trembling and quite unable to speak.

'Please, Margaret, most dear love, will not you take the ring?' he whispered.

'But ...'

'But what?'

'I — I have no right to it, sir,' she whispered very low, made timid by the look in his eyes.

'No right!' he exclaimed fiercely. 'No right! Of course you have the right! Am not I offering it to you? I tell you it is Her Ladyship's ring!'

'But — but — I am not — '

She did not manage to finish her protest, for the marquis stopped her in mid-sentence by bending his head and kissing her very forcibly. When he drew back his head he looked at her defiantly.

'Now say you cannot wear it!' he challenged.

He picked the ring out of her palm and took hold of her left hand.

'You would not refuse, Margaret?' he said wistfully. 'Surely you can not refuse me? I love you more than I thought it possible to love any woman, and I had hoped . . . '

Margaret stood on tiptoe and caressed Lord St George's cheek and touched his lips lightly with her own.

'I do, my lord, I do. I love you entirely. Indeed, I could *not* refuse to wear your ring.'

The marquis slipped the ring on to Margaret's finger, then kissed her hand.

'My lady,' he said softly and very tenderly; 'my very dear, only dear lady.'

A long time later they were still in the library, sitting side by side on one of the huge leather sofas.

'And when did you first come to know you loved me, my love?' Lord St George asked with tender anxiety.

'I suppose it must have been when I heard that you had departed into Oxfordshire with Lady Selina,' Margaret said with a smile. 'I know I felt quite horridly jealous.'

'Did you? Oh, I am so glad!' the marquis returned. 'But really you had no need, my love. I was only taking her to stay with friends. Oxford was going into Kent with Miss Allenham — I expect they will be married, by the by — and Selina wished to go to Woodstock immediately. I went to Berkeley Street after we returned from Court the other evening, and she heard of my plans then.'

'It seems to me, my lord,' Margaret said teasing him, 'that you took a great while to fetch the ring! It is no great journey into Oxfordshire, I think!'

The marquis looked chagrined.

'To tell you the truth, dear heart, it was a wasted journey!'

'When — you went to get this!' Margaret cried, looking down at the ring glittering on her finger. 'Oh, pray, my lord, do not say that!'

'No, no! I mean — the ring was not in Oxfordshire. I hunted high and low; I turned the house inside out, you have never seen such pandemonium! But it was not to be found. Then I bethought me that I must have left it in the safe-keeping of Howard, my lawyer. But he was at Banbury, on the other side of the county, and so I had to wait till he had returned. Only to find that he had not got it! I did not know what to do! For I had vowed to myself not to speak to you till I could place the ring upon your finger — as my father and grandfather had done with their wives before me. Then Howard, God bless him, remembered hearing me say that I would keep it at my bank here in London, so I came racing back last night, and pretty angry with myself, I can tell you! Wasting two whole days! Then, on top of everything, I had to wait till my bankers deigned to open this morning! More lost time!'

'So, you have had the ring ready to hand for some long time, my lord — ' Margaret teased.

'Never! Never had I any such thought!' Lord St George protested.

Margaret kissed his cheek.

'No matter, my lord! We have it safe here now. But why did not you mention on our return from Court that you were to depart into Oxfordshire?'

'I had not then quite decided. But when I left you and my aunt, I thought about Frampton and was certain he meant to speak. I remembered the way he looked at you; how he spoke to you! I would have to risk one day away . . .'

'And was that when you decided you loved me, my lord? When you thought Lord Frampton was about to — ?'

'Oh, no! I knew my heart long before! When my ward proposed to you, I felt all the impertinence of it! I knew then that you should not be wasted upon a mere boy!'

'But if I had accepted him, my lord — to be a duchess!'

'Then I should have forbidden the marriage! I should have exerted my powers as a guardian! Oh, I should not have let you marry anyone else upon any account!'

'But how did you come to change from thinking of me as a scheming, designing female, my lord, for that is certainly how you first regarded me, to someone who — '

'Never!' the marquis broke in. 'Never! I never did think of you so!' he protested vehemently.

'Oh, come, sir — !'

'No, certainly, I never did. It had been *put* to me that you were such, I admit, but the rumours did not fit you when I met you.'

'In spite of the Hellington pearls, and your ward, and Almack's and my clothes, and — everything?'

'In spite of *everything*!'

'It appeared quite otherwise, my lord!' Margaret giggled.

'And it was at Alamck's that I began to make the effort to win you,' Lord St George continued. 'Surely you must have seen that I was trying to be agreeable!'

'Indeed! Is that what it was, my lord! I thought you were being quite odiously satirical!'

'You perhaps do not realize, Miss Lambart,' the marquis said severely, 'how very like a naughty boy you have sometimes made me feel!'

'I do not believe it, sir!' Margaret protested laughing. 'I simply do not believe it!'

'You were exceedingly provoking, ma'am! Perhaps you do not realize how very thick you used to be with Brummell! You gave him all the smiles and confidences I wanted for myself. You made me suffer a great deal, ma'am!'

'If that be true, my lord, I have amply made up for it these last two days!'

And then the marquis kissed her again.

At that moment the door of the library opened a little and Lady Grampian's face peeped in.

'Are you — ?' she began, smiling.

'Oh, come in, Emma, do!' Lord St George said resignedly. 'How did you get here?'

'In my carriage, of course. Come in, Aunt James; they seem quite ready to receive our felicitations by the look of them!'

Margaret sprang to her feet as Lady Grampian held the door open for her aunt who came towards Margaret with her arms outstretched. The old lady embraced her warmly, glanced down at the huge diamond glinting on Margaret's finger, nodded her head, pleased, and kissed her goddaughter again.

'Oh, my dear,' she said unsteadily, 'you really have given me the most terrible two days!'

'I, ma'am!'

'I was quite terrified that you might accept Lord Frampton!'

'But — you did not say very much to dissuade me!'

'I knew St George must win you for himself! He would not have thanked me for interfering. Besides, opposition might have made Lord Frampton seem more attractive.'

Margaret laughed, while Lady James turned to embrace her nephew, and Emma turned from her brother to salute Margaret.

'I always told you, St George, that you should marry Margaret,' Lady Grampian said happily. 'I am so glad you have taken my advice. I am very thankful that I am to have such a sister at last. When I heard that you were gone into Oxfordshire with Selina, I thought you had taken leave of your senses! I was very much afraid that I would have to have Selina after all!'

'Never!' exclaimed the marquis.

'It would not have done at all!' exclaimed Lady James.

'I am so glad that we agree, ma'am,' Lady Grampian said. 'It has all turned out excellently. I vow, Margaret, I nearly died when you told me that Frampton had been already, before I could give you St George's note. Mind you,' she went on, turning accusing eyes to her brother, 'it was not much of a note; I expected something a great deal better. But Aunt James promised to keep Margaret occupied. Oh! I have just thought of something!' And Lady Grampian put her hand up to her mouth, her eyes sparkling impishly above. 'Perhaps Frampton would do for Selina. He will be upon the look-out again now — '

'Emma!' protested Margaret, laughing.

'It is not that I wish Selina any ill,' Lady Grampian went on fairly, 'but really she has been so horrid to you, Margaret, that I do not wish to see her take precedence of you, and Frampton is only an earl. Of course, she will be very polite in future, for she will certainly wish to be received in Oxfordshire.'

'Well, she will only be invited if Lady St George wishes it,' the marquis said firmly, with a tender glance at Margaret.

'And now we must begin to think about the wedding!' Lady James said happily as she sat down. 'Oh, all this is a very great deal better than I dared to hope when first you came to Hanover Square, my dear, with all that silly nonsense you had about not wanting to be married! I knew it would not last! And after only *one* season! It really is an excellent match!' She looked defiantly at her nephew. 'I always knew I should be very proud of you. I shall give you the Hellington pearls as your betrothal present!'

Margaret stared.

'But, ma'am, they are far too — ' she began.

'No! Not one word!' Lady James said firmly. 'I have always meant you to have them in any case. But living as you did in Cheshire, I never thought to have the pleasure of seeing you wear any of the pieces. And when you have them, you will be able to go to St George with some independence.'

And she looked defiantly at her nephew again.

Margaret kissed her godmother, quite unable to say more than 'Thank you'.

'Oh, I beg you, ma'am, do not encourage her,' the marquis said hurriedly. 'Miss Lambart has always felt a great deal too independent!'

'But there will be no more need for it now,' Margaret managed to say softly, with a tearful smile at St George.

It was at that moment that the great front door bell was heard again. This time the persons in the library took no notice of it, but Joshua appeared to announce that Sir Thomas and

Lady Pettigrew, Mr and Mrs James Thornton, and the Reverend Arthur and Mrs Temple were asking for Miss Lambart.

Margaret could have wished that her family had chosen any other time to call upon her, but Lady James exclaimed, 'Kindly show them in here, Joshua, they could not have chosen to come at a better time!'

The footman bowed, retired, and in another moment or two had flung the door open again, and was announcing the visitors in a booming voice.

Lady James received them, introduced herself, and performed the other introductions, leaving Margaret to collect herself.

'You have come at a most opportune moment,' Lady James decared. 'My nephew, the marquis and Miss Lambart are but just betrothed.'

Six pairs of eyes turned to Margaret and gazed at her in astonishment. As ever, Anne was the first to recover herself.

'Margaret, you sly creature!' she cried with a simpering laugh; 'you mentioned nothing of this!'

'I did not — ' began Margaret, but Anne's attention was already focussed upon her future brother-in-law.

'Oh, my lord! What can I say? This is indeed so utterly astonishing! My sister Margaret! Of all people! That you should wish to . . . Oh, it is quite beyond belief!'

'It is quite true, nevertheless, ma'am,' the marquis returned gravely. 'Miss Lambart has done me the great honour to consent to be my wife.'

Margaret did not hear any further exchange, for her other two sisters were embracing her and her brothers-in-law crowded about her also. Her youngest sister, Jane, so recently a bride herself, was clearly genuinely happy for her.

'Oh, Margaret!' she cried. 'Oh, this is wonderful news!'

Sarah was more practical.

'Fancy! You to be a peeress, Margaret! And a marchioness at that! I suppose you will become very grand now. I am sure I wish you all the happiness in the world, though I must say, this is something I never expected to witness!'

Like his wife, Sir Thomas was sincere in his felicitations, as was Mr Thornton, though for quite a different reason. His chief reaction was one of relief that he would never now have a spinster sister-in-law dependent upon him. He felt expansive enough because of this to be a great deal more generous in his felicitations than was his wife who, in between flattering speeches to the marquis, was confining herself to large expressions of surprise.

'My dear Margaret,' Mr Thornton now intoned,' you know that you and — er — the marquis will always be most welcome to visit us — whenever you like, and for as long as you like — er — you, and — er — his lordship — I have a good manor, you know; his — er — lordship might like to try my coverts some time.'

'Thank you, James; you are very kind.'

'Where — is St George's estate?' he demanded, looking suddenly anxious. 'He has a country seat, I collect? He is not one of these landless peers, is he?'

'Oh, no, James,' Margaret assured him wryly; 'you need have no worries over that. Lord St George has a property in Oxfordshire.'

'Ah, a very good county, very good,' James nodded approvingly. 'And — er — how large is it?'

'I am afraid I do not know, James. But I am quite sure it will cover quite enough acres to suit even a marquis's consequence,' Margaret replied innocently.

James Thornton looked at her suspiciously, not quite certain how to take her answer, but Margaret was now being kissed chastely by her brother-in-law, the cleric, and his powerful voice cut out all others.

'Now, of course, Margaret, you will

doubtless find yourself responsible for the moral welfare of a large household and estate. I am fully aware of your capacity for such work, but should you require advice — at any time — pray do not hesitate to call upon me, sister. Those of us who are called to an elevated position bear a great responsibility.'

'I will certainly remember your words, Arthur,' Margaret said calmly.

He went on to say a good deal more in the same vein, and Margaret was able to let her attention wander while the Reverend Arthur Temple enjoyed the sound of his own voice.

She looked at her family with detachment; it was strange how provincial they looked to her now, and she wondered that she had been able to bear their whims and their indifference so patiently and for so long. She found herself being immensely grateful that Oxfordshire was so far distant from Cheshire as it was. How pleasant it would have been to bring the marquis one kinswoman of undoubted congeniality!

The visitors stayed a long time: a very long time. They consumed a quantity of wine and cakes, and appeared as though they intended to take root in Lady James's library. In fact, it was only their hostess claiming an appointment that finally induced them to take their leave, promising to return upon the morrow.

'St George,' Lady James said when the four of them were alone again, 'I think I have a liking to try country air. Would it be convenient if Miss Lambart and I were to come to visit you in Oxfordshire for the remainder of the summer?'

The marquis stared at first.

'You — in the country, ma'am!'

'Yes. I cannot see any purpose in remaining here longer; I have done all that a lady presenting a young girl should do, and it is nearly August. Of course, if you have other plans — '

'Oh, no, ma'am; I should be delighted to receive you.'

'Good. Then I shall go and pay a few calls; I have several friends whom I know will wish to congratulate me.'

And with that, she kissed Margaret, allowed Lady Grampian and St George to kiss her, and went out.

'I suppose you would like me to go also, St George,' laughed Lady Grampian. 'Well, I shall not remain to be a gooseberry. Goodbye, dearest Margaret; there is nothing in the world that could have made me happier!'

And kissing her brother and her future sister-in-law lightly, she hurried away.

St George and Margaret looked at each other. Margaret smiled ruefully.

'We need never venture into Cheshire, my lord,' she said.

Lady Grampian put her head round the door.

'I am just going to write to Selina to tell her the news. What a pity I shall not be there when she receives my letter!'

And Lady Grampian's head withdrew

and the door closed again.

The lovers looked at each other and laughed.

'My dearest, you see, all families have their cross to bear! And there will be no need for you to invite her into Oxfordshire if you do not choose!'

Margaret looked at St George fondly.

'I shall be happy to share this cross with you also, my lord, as indeed I shall all things!'

THE END

Other titles in the Linford Romance Library

SAVAGE PARADISE
Sheila Belshaw

For four years, Diana Hamilton had dreamed of returning to Luangwa Valley in Zambia. Now she was back — and, after a close encounter with a rhino — was receiving a lecture from a tall, khaki-clad man on the dangers of going into the bush alone!

PAST BETRAYALS
Giulia Gray

As soon as Jon realized that Julia had fallen in love with him, he broke off their relationship and returned to work in the Middle East. When Jon's best friend, Danny, proposed a marriage of friendship, Julia accepted. Then Jon returned and Julia discovered her love for him remained unchanged.

PRETTY MAIDS ALL IN A ROW
Rose Meadows

The six beautiful daughters of George III of England dreamt of handsome princes coming to claim them, but the King always found some excuse to reject proposals of marriage. This is the story of what befell the Princesses as they began to seek lovers at their father's court, leaving behind rumours of secret marriages and illegitimate children.

THE GOLDEN GIRL
Paula Lindsay

Sarah had everything — wealth, social background, great beauty and magnetic charm. Her heart was ruled by love and compassion for the less fortunate in life. Yet, when one man's happiness was at stake, she failed him — and herself.

A DREAM OF HER OWN
Barbara Best

A stranger gently kisses Sarah Danbury at her Betrothal Ball. Little does she realise that she is to meet this mysterious man again in very different circumstances.

HOSTAGE OF LOVE
Nara Lake

From the moment pretty Emma Tregear, the only child of a Van Diemen's Land magnate, met Philip Despard, she was desperately in love. Unfortunately, handsome Philip was a convict on parole.

THE ROAD TO BENDOUR
Joyce Eaglestone

Mary Mackenzie had lived a sheltered life on the family farm in Scotland. When she took a job in the city she was soon in a romantic maze from which only she could find the way out.

NEW BEGINNINGS
Ann Jennings

On the plane to his new job in a hospital in Turkey, Felix asked Harriet to put their engagement on hold, as Philippe Krir, the Director of Bodrum hospital, refused to hire 'attached' people. But, without an engagement ring, what possible excuse did Harriet have for holding Philippe at bay?

THE CAPTAIN'S LADY
Rachelle Edwards

1820: When Lianne Vernon becomes governess at Elswick Manor, she finds her young pupil is given to strange imaginings and that her employer, Captain Gideon Lang, is the most enigmatic man she has ever encountered. Soon Lianne begins to fear for her pupil's safety.

THE VAUGHAN PRIDE
Margaret Miles

As the new owner of Southwood Manor, Laura Vaughan discovers that she's even more poverty stricken than before. She also finds that her neighbour, the handsome Marius Kerr, is a little too close for comfort.

HONEY-POT
Mira Stables

Lovely, well-born, well-dowered, Russet Ingram drew all men to her. Yet here she was, a prisoner of the one man immune to her graces — accused of frivolously tampering with his young ward's romance!

DREAM OF LOVE
Helen McCabe

When there is a break-in at the art gallery she runs, Jade can't believe that Corin Bossinney is a trickster, or that she'd fallen for the oldest trick in the book . . .

FOR LOVE OF OLIVER
...ncey

Whe... ...er family
home, ... block
from which she runs ... riding
school. But she soon discovers
Oliver is not an easy neighbour
to have. Then Carly is presented
with a new challenge, one she must
face for love of Oliver.

THE SECRET OF
MONKS' HOUSE
Rachelle Edwards

Soon after her arrival at Monks'
House, Lilith had been told that
it was haunted by a monk, and
she had laughed. Of greater interest
was their neighbour, the mysterious
Fabian Delamaye. Was he truly as
debauched as rumour told, and
what was the truth about his wife's
death?